ARSÈNE LUPIN INTERVENES

ARSÈNE LUPIN INTERVENES

MAURICE LE BLANC

WILDSIDE PRESS

CHAPTER I

FOREWORD

Contrary, perhaps, to the opinion of the Bright Young People in our midst, the World-before-the-War was not by any means barren of adventure and excitement. Only, they did things differently then. There was, in those days, a certain sparkling gaiety, a spontaneity, a *chic* sadly lacking from the exploits of a younger generation. There was wit as well as honor among thieves. Just as really good wine differs from that modern depravity, the cocktail, so does the finished artistry of Jim Barnett compare with the outrages of bobbed-hair bandits and cat-burglars.

For Barnett had a brain and used it; a sense of humor, and rejoiced in it. He was independent of revolvers and racing cars and hypodermic syringes. He made a confidant of no man—or woman. He was an unassisted conjurer, as it were, performing his little tricks always in the full glare of the limelight, relying entirely on his own lightning skill to vanish his watches and evolve his rabbits.

A curious, memorable figure, Jim Barnett. By profession, a private detective, principal of the Barnett Agency in the *rue Laborde*, with a modest ground-floor office for his headquarters. Unlike others of his trade, he worked entirely alone. He employed no spies, and saved himself their possible treachery. He had no secretary for the simple reason that he kept no records. His telephone rang infrequently, and when it did he answered it himself.

In appearance, Barnett was something of a problem. He gave the impression of a man who is wilfully badly dressed, intentionally careless of his attire. His coat's sole claim to respect was its indubitable antiquity. His trousers—but we will spare possible heartbreak to the tailors who read this description. He wore his incongruous monocle like some exotic bloom—its startling aristocracy in conjunction with the rest of his get-up was that of an orchid in an onion patch.

What a contrast to his friend, Inspector Béchoux, that immaculate sprig of the Paris Police Force. Béchoux was frankly a dandy, devoting all his off-time to the adornment of his person. Yet he was no fool. Only, his brain moved in the channels of detective routine, whereas Barnett's leaped nimbly from point to point of a mystery until it plucked out the heart.

Be it said to Inspector Béchoux's undying honor that he recognized Barnett's gifts quite openly. He even resorted to asking his help in various problems, and it is the inner history of some of these that this book now reveals for the first time to the world at large.

The peculiar feature of all the Béchoux-Barnett cases was always either their apparent insolubility (*e.g.*, the Disappearance of the Twelve Little Nigger Boys) or the fact that they seemed solved at the outset (as in the case of the Man with the Gold Teeth). And the finale of each presented certain similar features—a dramatic and quite unexpected eleventh-hour *dénouement*; a swift adjustment of account between the innocent and guilty parties; *and* —a highly satisfactory windfall for Barnett. Only, as Inspector Béchoux bitterly observed, it was always the kind of windfall that meant shaking the tree. Barnett's gifts would have stripped an orchard....

What placed Inspector Béchoux in a serious dilemma was that in every case Barnett's position was unassailable from start to finish. His victims were people who could not be brought to speak a word against him. You could call it intimidation—blackmail—what you liked. Barnett merely grinned and fed large checks to his banking account.

Large checks—and yet the slogan of the Barnett Agency was:—

"Information Free. No Fees of Any Kind."

Which was paradoxically true. Barnett's income was composed not of fees but of levies. Sometimes he took toll of his clients, sometimes of their enemies. A certain poetic justice characterized his depredations. The poor and the innocent had nothing to fear from Jim Barnett.

And he was undeniably on the side of the law so far as results went. Only, where it suited his purpose, he meted out his own idea of a suitable punishment to criminals instead of turning them over to the police.

Inspector Béchoux was probably Barnett's only close friend. Yet all he knew of him was gleaned from the hours they spent together when Barnett intervened in one of his cases. He was quite ignorant of Barnett's private life—his antecedents—even his identity. For there was always one mystery which remained unsolved. Who was the man who called himself "Jim Barnett"?

There was something about his methods and his amusing buffoonery which could not fail to recall the King of Crooks—the one man who persisted in eluding and baffling the Paris police—the man Inspector Béchoux would have given his life-savings to lay hands on—whom he sometimes, in his inmost heart, half suspected to be masquerading as "Barnett," and then dismissed the suspicion as fantastic.

4

It is a long way back to pre-war Paris, and the clash of wits between Barnett and Inspector Béchoux. In these days, when so much of admiration and adulation is being misapplied, honor to whom honor is due! The moment has come when we can openly state that the worthy Inspector's instinct was right, and the "interventions" of Jim Barnett may safely be attributed to their perpetrator—Arsène Lupin!

CHAPTER II

"DROPS THAT TRICKLE AWAY...."

The courtyard bell, on the ground floor of the Baronne Assermann's imposing residence in the Faubourg St. Germain, rang loudly, and a moment later the maid brought in an envelope.

"The gentleman says he has an appointment with madame for four o'clock."

Madame Assermann slit the envelope. Taking out a card, she held it gingerly between her fingertips, and read:

The Barnett Agency

Information Free

"Show the gentleman into my boudoir," she drawled.

Valérie Assermann—the beautiful Valérie she had been called for some thirty years—still retained a measure of good looks, although she was now thick-set, past middle-age and elaborately made-up. Her haughty and at times harsh expression had yet a certain candor which was not without charm.

As the wife of Assermann, the banker, she took pride in her vast house with its luxurious appointments, in her large circle of acquaintances and in all the pomp and circumstance of her social position. Behind her back society gossips whispered that Valérie had been guilty of various rather more than trifling indiscretions. Even hardened Parisian scandalmongers professed themselves shocked at her behavior. There were those who suggested that the baron, an ailing old man, had contemplated getting a divorce.

Baron Assermann had been confined to his bed for several weeks with heart trouble, and Valérie rearranged the pillows under his thin shoulders and asked him, rather absent-mindedly, how he was feeling, before proceeding to her boudoir.

Awaiting her there she found a curious person—a sturdily built, square-shouldered man, well set up, but shockingly dressed in a funereal frock-coat, moth-eaten and shiny, which hung in depressed creases over worn, baggy trousers. His face was young, but the rugged energy of his features was spoiled by a coarse, blotchy skin, almost brick-red in tone. Behind the monocle, which he used for either eye indifferently, his cold and rather mocking glance sparkled with a boyish gaiety.

"Mr. Barrett?" Valérie asked, on a rising inflection, making no effort to keep the scorn out of her voice.

He bowed, and, before she could withdraw it, he had kissed her hand with a flourish, following this gallantry by a not quite inaudible click of the tongue—suggesting his appreciation of the perfumed flavor.

"Jim Barnett—at your service, madame la baronne. When I got your letter I stopped just long enough to give my coat a brush … that was all.…"

The baronne wondered for a moment whether she should show her visitor the door, but he faced her with all the composure of a man of rank, and, a little taken aback, she merely said:

"I've been told that you are quite clever at disentangling rather delicate and complicated matters.…"

He gave a self-satisfied smirk.

"Yes—I've rather a gift for seeing clearly; seeing *through* and *into* things—and people."

While his voice was soft, his tone was masterful and his whole demeanor conveyed a suggestion of veiled irony. He seemed so sure of himself and his powers that it was impossible not to share his confidence, and Valérie felt herself coming under the influence of this unknown common detective, this head of a private inquiry bureau. Resenting the feeling, she interrupted him:

"Perhaps we had better—er—discuss terms.…"

"Quite unnecessary," replied Barnett.

"But surely"—it was she who was smiling now—"you do not work merely for glory?"

"The services of the Barnett Agency, madame la baronne, are entirely free."

She looked disappointed, and insisted: "I should prefer to arrange some remuneration—your out-of-pocket expenses, at least."

"A tip?" he sneered.

She flushed angrily. Her satin-shod foot tapped the carpet.

"I cannot possibly …" she began.

"Be under an obligation to me? Don't worry, madame la baronne, I shall see to it that we end up quits for whatever slight service I may be able to render you."

Was there a note of menace in the suave voice?

Valérie shuddered a trifle uneasily. What was the meaning of this obscure remark? How did this man propose to recoup himself? Really, this Jim Barnett aroused in her almost the same sort of dread, the same queer kind of nightmare emotion that one might feel if suddenly confronted with a burglar! He might even be … yes, he was quite possibly some undesirable, unknown admirer. She wondered what she had better do. Ring for her maid? But he had so far dominated her that, regardless of the consequences, she found herself submitting passively to his questioning as to what had caused her to apply to his agency. Her account was brief, as Barnett seemed to be in a hurry, and she spoke frankly and to the point.

"It all happened the Sunday before last," she began. "After a game of bridge with some friends, I went to bed rather early and fell asleep as usual. About four o'clock—at ten minutes past, to be exact—a noise woke me and then I heard a bang which sounded to me like a door closing. It came from my boudoir—this room we are in, which communicates with my bedroom and also with a corridor leading to the servants' staircase. I'm not nervous, so after a moment's hesitation I got up, came in here and turned on the light. The room was empty, but this small show-case"—she indicated it —"had fallen down, and several of the curios and statuettes in it were broken. I then went to my husband's room and found him reading in bed; he said he had heard nothing. He was very much upset and rang for the butler, who immediately made a thorough search of the house. In the morning we called in the police."

"And the result?" asked Barnett.

"They could find no trace of the arrival or departure of any intruder. How he entered and got away is a mystery. But under a footstool among the débris of the curios some one found half a candle, and an awl set in a very dirty wooden handle. Now on the previous afternoon a plumber had been to repair the taps of the washbasin in my husband's dressing-room. The man's employer, when questioned, identified the tool and, moreover, the other half of the candle was found in his shop."

"On that point, then," interrupted Jim Barnett, "you have definite evidence."

"Yes, but against that is the indisputable and disconcerting fact that the investigation also proved that the workman in question took the six o'clock express to Brussels, arriving there at midnight—four hours before the disturbance which awakened me."

"Really? Has the man returned?"

"No. They lost track of him at Antwerp, where he was spending money lavishly."

"Is that all you can tell me?"

"Absolutely all."

"Who's been in charge of this investigation?"

"Inspector Béchoux."

"What! The worthy Béchoux! He's a very good friend of mine. We've often worked together."

"It was he who mentioned your Agency."

"Yes, because he'd come up against a blank wall, I suppose."

Barnett crossed to the window and leaning his head against the pane thought hard for a few minutes, frowning ponderously and whistling under his breath. Then he returned to Madame Assermann and continued:

"You and Béchoux, madame, conclude that this was an attempted burglary. Am I right?"

"Yes. An unsuccessful attempt, since nothing has been taken."

"That's so. But all the same there must have been a definite motive behind this attempt. What was it?"

Valérie hesitated. "I really don't know," she said after a moment. But again her foot tapped restlessly.

The detective shrugged his shoulders; then, pointing to one of the silk-draped panels which lined the boudoir above the wainscoting he asked:

"What's under that panel?"

"I beg your pardon," she said in some bewilderment; "what do you mean?"

"I mean that the most superficial observation reveals the fact that the edges of that silk oblong are slightly frayed, and here and there they are separated from the woodwork by a slit: there is every reason to suppose that a safe is concealed there."

Valérie gave a start. How on earth could the man have guessed from such imperceptible indications.... Then with a jerk she slid the panel open, disclosing a small steel door. As she feverishly worked the three knobs of the safe an unreasoning fear came over her. Impossible as the hypothesis seemed, she wondered whether this queer stranger might somehow have robbed her during the few minutes he had been left alone in the room!

At length, taking a key from her pocket, she opened the safe, and gave a sigh of relief. There it was—the only object the safe contained—a magnificent pearl necklace. Seizing it quickly, she twined its triple strands round her wrist.

Barnett laughed.

"Easier in your mind now, madame la baronne? Yes, it's quite a pretty piece of jewelry, and I can understand its having been stolen from you."

"But it's not been stolen," she protested. "Even if the thief was after this, he failed to steal it."

"Do you really think so?"

"Of course. Here is the necklace in my hands. When anything's stolen it disappears. Well—here it is...."

"Here's *a* necklace," he corrected her quietly; "but are you sure that it is *your* necklace and that it has any value?"

9

"What *do* you mean?" she asked in unconcealed annoyance. "Only a fortnight ago my jeweller valued it at half a million francs."

"A fortnight ago—that is to say, five days before that night.... And now? Please remember I know nothing; I have not valued the necklace; it is merely a supposition. But are you yourself entirely without suspicion?"

Valérie stood quite still. What suspicion was he hinting at? In what connection? A vague anxiety crept over her as his suggestion persisted. As she weighed the mass of heaped-up pearls in her outstretched hand it seemed to get lighter and lighter. As she looked she discovered variations in coloring, unaccustomed reflections, a disturbing unevenness, a changed graduation— each detail more disturbing than the last, until in the back of her mind the terrible truth began to dawn, distinct and threatening.

Jim Barnett gave vent to a short chuckle.

"Just so. You're getting there, are you? On the right track at last—one more mental effort and all is clear as day! It's all quite logical. Your enemy doesn't just steal—he substitutes. Nothing disappears, and except for the noise of the falling show-case everything would have been carried out in perfect secrecy and have gone undiscovered. Until some fresh development occurred, you would have been absolutely unaware that the real necklace had vanished and that you were displaying on your snowy shoulders a string of imitation pearls."

Valérie was so absorbed in her own thoughts that she hardly noticed the familiarity of the man's words and manner.

Barnett leaned towards her.

"Well—that settles the first point. And now we know what he stole, let's look for the thief. That's the procedure in all well-conducted cases. And once we've found the thief we shan't be far from recovering the object of the theft."

He gave Valérie's hand a friendly pat of reassurance.

"Cheer up, madame. We're on the right scent now. Let's begin by a little guesswork—it's an excellent method. We'll suppose that your husband, in spite of his illness, had sufficient strength to drag himself from his own room to this one, armed with the candle, and, anyway, with the tool the plumber left behind; we'll go on to suppose that he opened the safe, clumsily overturned the show-case and then fled in case you had heard the noise. Doesn't that throw a little light on it all? How naturally it accounts for the absence of any trace of arrival or departure, and also for the safe being opened without being forced, since Baron Assermann must many a time in all these years have come in here with you in the evening, seen you work the lock, noted the clicks and intervals and counted the number of notches displaced—and so, gradually, have discovered the three letters of the cipher."

This "little guesswork," as Jim Barnett termed it, seemed to appall the beautiful Valérie as he went on "supposing" step by step. It was as if she saw it all happening before her eyes. At last she stammered out distractedly:

"What you suggest is madness. You don't suppose my husband.... If someone came here that night, it couldn't have been the baron. Don't be absurd!"

"Did you have a copy of your necklace?" he interjected.

She paused. When she spoke it was slowly, with forced calm.

"Yes ... my husband ordered one, for safety, when we bought it—four years ago."

"And where is the copy?"

"My husband kept it," she replied, her voice a mere whisper.

"Well," said Barnett cheerfully, "that's the copy you've got in your hands; he has substituted it for the real pearls which he has taken. As for his motive—well, since his fortune places Baron Assermann above any suspicion of theft, we must look for something more intimate ... more subtle.... Revenge? A desire to torture—to injure—perhaps to punish? What do you think yourself? After all, a young and pretty woman's rather reckless behavior may be very understandable, but her husband is bound to judge it fairly severely.... Forgive me, madame. I have no right to pry into the secrets of your private life. I am merely here to locate, with your help, the present whereabouts of your necklace."

"No," cried Valérie, starting back. "No!"

Suddenly she felt she could no longer endure this ally who, in the course of a brief, friendly, almost frivolous conversation, had fathomed with diabolical ease all the secret circumstances of her life by a method quite unlike the ordinary methods employed by the police. And this man was now pointing out with an air of good-natured banter the precipice to whose edge fate seemed to be forcing her.

The sound of his sarcastic voice became all at once intolerable. She hated the mere thought of his searching for her necklace.

"No," she repeatedly obstinately.

He bowed, insolently servile.

"As you wish, madame. I have not the slightest desire to seem importunate. I am simply here to serve you in so far as you want my help. Besides, as things are now, you can safely dispense with my aid, since your husband is quite unfit to go out and will scarcely have been so imprudent as to entrust the pearls to any one else. If you make a careful search, you will probably discover them hidden somewhere in his room. I need say no more—except that if you should need me, telephone me at my office between nine and ten any night. And now I respectfully withdraw, madame la baronne."

Again he kissed her hand and she dared not resist him. Then he took his leave jauntily, swinging along with an irritating air of utter complacency. The courtyard gate clanged behind him. To Valérie it brought a curious premonition of doom—as if a prison gate had now closed upon her.

That evening, Valérie summoned Inspector Béchoux, whose continued attendance seemed only natural, and the search began.

Béchoux, a conscientious detective and a pupil of the famous Canimard, adhered to the approved methods of his profession—and proceeded to examine the baron's bathroom and private study in sections. After all, a necklace with three strands of pearls is too large an object for it to remain hidden from an expert searcher for very long. Nevertheless, after a week's persistent search, including several night visits when, owing to the baron's habit of taking sleeping draughts, he was able to examine even the bed and the bedclothes, Béchoux admitted himself discouraged. The necklace could not possibly be in the house.

In spite of her instinctive aversion, Valérie was tempted to get in touch once more with the impossible man at the Barnett Agency. Despite the repugnance with which he inspired her, she felt positive he would know how to perform the miracle of finding the necklace.

Then matters were brought to a head by a crisis which came suddenly, though not unexpectedly. One evening the servants summoned their mistress hastily—the baron lay choking and prostrate on a divan near the bathroom door. His distorted features and the anguish in his eyes were indicative of the most acute suffering.

Almost paralyzed with fright, Valérie was about to telephone for the doctor, but the baron stammered out the words, "Too late … it's … too … late…."

Then, trying to rise, he gasped out: "A drink …" and would have staggered to the washstand.

Quickly Valérie thrust him back on to the divan.

"There's water here in the carafe," she urged.

"No.… I want it … from the tap.…" He fell back, exhausted.

She turned on the tap quickly, fetched a glass and filled it, but when she took it to him, he would not drink.

There was a long silence except for the sound of the water running in the basin. The dying man's face became drawn and sunken. He motioned to his wife and she leaned forward—but, doubtless to prevent the servants hearing, he repeated the word "closer," and again "closer."

Valérie hesitated, as though afraid of what he might want to say, but his imperious glance cowed her and she knelt down with her ear almost touching his lips. Then he whispered, incoherently, and she could scarcely so much as guess what the words meant.

"The pearls ... the necklace ... you shall know before I'm gone ... you never loved me ... you married me ... for ... my money...."

She began to protest indignantly at his making such a cruel accusation at this solemn moment, but he seized her wrist and repeated in a kind of confused delirium: "... for my money, and your conduct has proved it. You have never been a good wife to me—that's why I wanted to punish you—why I'm punishing you now—it's an exquisite joy—the only pleasure possible to me—and I can die happily now because the pearls are vanishing away.... Can't you hear them, falling, dropping away into the swirling water. Ah, Valérie, my wife ... what a punishment! ... the drops that trickle away!..."

His strength failed him again, and the servants lifted him onto his bed. The doctor came very soon after, and two elderly spinster cousins who had been summoned settled themselves in the room and refused to budge. The final paroxysm was prolonged and painful. At dawn Baron Assermann died, without uttering another word.

At the formal request of the cousins, a seal was placed on every drawer and cupboard in the room. Then the long death vigil began....

Two days later, after the funeral, the dead man's lawyer called and asked to speak to Valérie in private. He looked grave and troubled and said at once:

"Madame, I have a most painful duty to perform, and I prefer to get it over as quickly as possible, while assuring you beforehand that the injustice done to you was subject to my profound disapproval and contrary to my advice and entreaty. But it was useless to oppose an unshakable determination...."

"I beg you, monsieur," stammered Valérie, "to make your meaning clear."

"I am coming to it, madame la baronne—it is this. I hold a will drawn up by Baron Assermann twenty years ago, appointing you his sole heiress and residuary legatee. But I have to tell you that last month the baron confided to me that he had made a fresh will ... by which he left his entire fortune to his two cousins...."

"He made a new will?" cried Valérie.

"Yes."

"And you have it?"

"After reading it to me he locked it in that desk. He did not wish it to be read until a week after his death. It may not be unsealed before that date."

Now Valérie realized why, a few years before, after a series of violent quarrels, her husband had advised her to sell all her own jewelry and purchase a pearl necklace with the money. Disinherited, with no fortune of her

13

own, and with an imitation pearl necklace in place of the real one, she was left penniless.

The day before the seals were to be broken, a car drew up in the *rue Laborde* in front of rather dingy premises bearing the sign:

THE BARNETT AGENCY
Open from Two to Three
Information Free

A veiled woman in deep mourning got out of the car and knocked on the glass panel of the inner door.

"Come in," called a voice from within.

She entered.

"Who's that," went on the voice in the back room, which was separated from the office by a curtain. She recognized the tones.

"Baronne Assermann," she replied.

"Excuse me, madame. Please take a seat. I won't keep you a moment."

While she waited, Valérie looked round the office. It was comparatively empty; the furniture consisted of a table and two old armchairs. The walls were quite bare and the place was innocent of files or papers. A telephone was the only indication of activity. An ash-tray, however, held the stubs of several expensive cigarettes, and a subtle fragrance hung in the air.

The curtain swung back and Jim Barnett appeared suddenly, alert and smiling. He wore the same shabby frock-coat, the same impossible, made-up tie, the same monocle at the end of a black ribbon.

He seized and kissed his visitor's gloved hand.

"How do you do, madame. This is indeed a pleasure. But what's the matter? I see you are in mourning—nothing serious, I hope—oh, but how absent-minded I am—of course—Baron Assermann, was it not? So sad! A charming man, and such a devoted husband. I should so much have liked to meet him. Well, well. Let's see—how did matters stand?"

As he spoke, he took from his pocket a slender note-book which he fingered pensively.

"Baronne Assermann—here we are—I remember. Imitation pearls—husband the thief—pretty woman.... A very pretty woman.... She is to telephone me.... Well, dear lady," he concluded, with increasing familiarity, "I am still awaiting that telephone call."

Once more, Valérie felt disconcerted by this man. Without wishing to pretend overwhelming sorrow at the death of her husband, she yet felt sad, and mingled with her sadness was a haunting dread of future poverty. She had had a bad time during the last days—and her wan face showed the ravages of terror and futile remorse resulting from her nightmare visions of ruin and distress.... And here was this impertinent upstart detective, not seeming to grasp the position at all....

With great dignity she recounted all that had happened, and although she avoided idle recriminations, she repeated what her husband's lawyer had said.

"Ah, yes; quite so," interposed the detective, smiling approval. "Good ... that all fits in admirably. It's quite a pleasure to see how logically this enthralling and well constructed drama is working itself out."

"A pleasure?" asked Valérie tonelessly.

"Certainly—a pleasure which my friend Inspector Béchoux must have enjoyed—for I suppose he's explained to you...."

"What?"

"What? Why, the key to the mystery, of course. Isn't it priceless? Old Béchoux must have rocked with mirth!"

Jim Barnett, at any rate, was laughing heartily.

"That washbasin trick now—there's a novelty! It's certainly farcical rather than dramatic—but so adroitly worked in—of course I spotted the dodge at once when you told me about the plumber, and saw the connection between the repairing of the washbasin and the baron's little plans. That was the crux of the whole thing. When he planned the substitution of the false necklace, your husband arranged a good hiding-place for the real pearls; it was essential for his purpose. Merely to deprive you of them and throw them or cause them to be thrown into the Seine like worthless rubbish, would only have been half a revenge. For it to be complete and on the grand scale he had to keep them close at hand, hidden in a spot at once near and inaccessible. And that's what he did."

Jim Barnett was thoroughly enjoying himself and went on jocularly: "Can't you imagine your husband explaining it all to the plumber? 'See here, my man, just examine that waste-pipe under my washbasin. It goes down to the wainscoting and leaves the bathroom at an almost imperceptible gradient, doesn't it? Well, reduce that gradient still more—take up the pipe in this dark corner, so as to form a sort of pocket—a blind alley, where something could be lodged if necessary. When the tap is turned on the water will fill the pocket and carry away the object lodged there. You understand? Then drill a hole about half an inch in diameter in the wall side of the pipe, where it won't be noticed. Yes—there! Done it? Now plug it up with this rubber stopper. Does it fit? That's all right then. Now, you understand, don't you—not a word to anyone! Keep your mouth shut. Take this and catch the Brussels express tonight. These three checks you can cash there—one every month. In three months' time you may come back to Paris. Good-bye. That's all, thanks.'... And that very night you heard a noise in your boudoir, the imitation pearls were substituted for the real

15

ones, and the latter secreted in the hiding-place prepared for them in the pocket of the pipe. Now do you see? Believing that the end has come, the baron calls out to you: 'A glass of water—not from the carafe—from the tap there.' You obey. And the terrible punishment is brought about by your own hand as it turns on the tap—the water runs, carries away the pearls, and the baron stammers out: 'Do you hear? They're trickling away—away!'"

The baronne listened in distracted silence. What impressed her most in Burnett's terrible story was not the full revelation of her husband's rancor and hatred, but the one fact which it hammered home.

"Then you knew the truth?" she murmured at last.

"Of course," he replied, "it's my job. The Barnett Agency, you see...."

"And you said nothing of this to me?" Her tone was an accusation.

"But, my dear baronne, it was you yourself who stopped me from telling you what I knew, or was just about to discover. You dismissed me—somewhat peremptorily, I fear—and not wishing to be thought officious, I did not press the matter. Besides, I had still to verify my deductions."

"And have you done so?" she faltered.

"Yes. Just out of curiosity, that's all."

"When?"

"The same night."

"What! You got into the house that night—into our rooms? I heard nothing...."

"Oh, I've a little way of working on the quiet.... Even Baron Assermann didn't hear me. And yet...."

"What?..."

"Well, just to make sure, I enlarged that hole, you see ... the one through which he had pushed the pearls into the pipe."

She started.

"Then you saw them?..."

"I did."

"My pearls were actually there?"

He nodded.

Valérie choked, as she repeated under her breath: "My pearls were there in the pipe and you could have taken them?..."

"Yes," he admitted nonchalantly, "and I really believe that but for me, Jim Barnett, at your service, they would have dropped away as the baron intended they should on the day of his death, which he knew was not far off. What were his words: 'They're vanishing ... can't you hear them? ... drops that trickle away ...!' And his plan of revenge would have come off—too bad—such a beautiful necklace—quite a collector's piece!"

Valérie was not given to violent explosions of wrath, likely to upset her complexion. But at this point she was worked up to such a pitch that she rushed up to Barnett and convulsively seized the collar of his coat.

"It's theft! You're a common adventurer! I suspected it all along—a crook!"

At the word "crook" the young man hooted with joy.

"I—a crook? How frightfully amusing!"

She took no notice. Shaking with passion, she rushed up and down the room shrieking: "I won't have it, I tell you. Give me back my pearls at once or I'll call the police!"

"Oh—how ugly that sounds," he exclaimed, "and how tactless for a pretty woman like yourself to behave like this to a man who has shown himself assiduous in serving you and only wants to coöperate peaceably with you for your good!"

She shrugged her shoulders and demanded again: "Will you give me my necklace?"

"Of course! it's absolutely at your disposal. Good heavens, do you suppose that Jim Barnett robs the people who pay him the compliment of seeking his help! What do you think would become of the Barnett Agency, which owes its popularity to its reputation for absolute integrity and disinterested service? I don't ask my clients for a single penny. If I kept your pearls I should be a thief—a crook, as you would say—whereas I am an honest man. Here, dear lady, is your necklace."

He produced a small cloth bag containing the rescued pearls and laid it on the table.

Thunderstruck, Valérie seized the precious necklace with shaking hands. She could hardly believe her eyes; it seemed incredible that this man should restore her property in this way, and with a sudden fear lest he was merely acting on a momentary impulse, she made abruptly for the door without a word of thanks.

"You're in rather a hurry all at once," laughed Jim Barnett. "Aren't you going to count them? Three hundred and forty-five. They're all there ... and they're the real ones, this time."

"Yes," said Valérie, "I know that...."

"You're quite sure? Those really are the pearls your jeweller valued at five hundred thousand francs?"

"Yes; they are the ones."

"You'd swear to that?"

"Certainly," she said positively.

"In that case, I'll buy them from you."

"You'll buy them! What do you mean?"

17

"Well, being penniless, you've got to sell them. Why not to me, then, since I can offer you more than anyone else will—I'll give you twenty times their value. Instead of five hundred thousand francs, I'll give ten million. Does that startle you? Ten million's a pretty figure."

"Ten million!"

"Exactly the reputed gross amount of the baron's estate."

Valérie lingered at the door, her fingers twisting the handle.

"My husband's estate," she repeated. "I don't see any connection. Please explain."

With gentle emphasis Jim Barnett continued: "It's very simple. You have your choice—the pearl necklace or the estate!"

"The pearl necklace ... the estate?" she repeated, puzzled.

"Certainly. As you yourself told me, the inheritance turns on two wills: the earlier one in your favor and the second in favor of those two old cousins, who are as rich as Crœsus and apparently correspondingly mean. But suppose Will Number Two can't be found, Will Number One is valid."

"But to-morrow," she said in faltering accents, "they intend to break the seals and open the desk—and the second will is there."

"The will may be there—or it may not," suggested Barnett, rather contemptuously. "I'll go so far as to say that in my humble opinion it is not."

"Is that possible?" she asked, staring at him in amazement.

"Quite possible—even probable—in fact, I seem to remember now that when I came to investigate the waste-pipe the evening after our talk, I took the opportunity of looking round your husband's rooms as he was sleeping so soundly."

"And you took that will," she asked haltingly.

"This rather looks like it, doesn't it?"

He unfolded a sheet of stamped paper and she recognized her husband's writing as she caught sight of the words: "*I, the undersigned, Léon Joseph Assermann, banker, in view of certain facts well known to her, do hereby declare that my wife Valérie Assermann shall not have the slightest claim upon my fortune and that....*"

She read no further. Her voice caught in her throat and falling limply into an armchair she gasped:

"You stole that paper—and expect me to be your accomplice.... I won't. My poor husband's wishes must be obeyed...."

Jim Barnett threw up his hands enthusiastically.

"How splendid of you, dear lady. Duty points to self-sacrifice, and I commend you the more when your lot is so especially hard—when for two old cousins who are quite undeserving of pity, you are prepared to sacrifice yourself with your own hands to gratify Baron Assermann's petty spite. You bow to this injustice to expiate those youthful peccadilloes. The beautiful

Valérie is to forego the luxury to which she is entitled and be reduced to abject poverty. But, before you finally make this choice, madame, I beg you to weigh your decision carefully and realize all it means. Let me be quite plain: *if that necklace leaves this room*, the lawyer receives Will Number Two tomorrow morning and you are disinherited."

"And if it stays?"

"Well, there's no will in that desk and you inherit the whole estate—ten million francs in your pocket, thanks to Jim Barnett."

His sarcasm was obvious, and Valérie felt like a helpless animal trapped in his ruthless grasp. There was no way out. If she refused him the necklace, the will would be read out next day. He was relentless, and would turn a deaf ear to any entreaties.

He stepped into the back room for a moment and then returned from behind the curtain, calmly wiping off his face the grease paint with which he had covered it, like an actor removing his make-up. His appearance was now completely changed—his face was fresh and young-looking, with a smooth, healthy skin. A fashionable tie had replaced the made-up atrocity. He had changed the old frock-coat and baggy trousers for a well-cut lounge suit. And his attitude of smiling confidence made it clear he did not fear denunciation or betrayal. In return, Valérie knew he would never say a word to anyone, even to Inspector Béchoux—the secret would be kept inviolate.

He leaned towards her and, laughing, said: "Well—I believe you're looking at it more reasonably now. That's good! Besides, who'll know that the wealthy Baronne Assermann is wearing imitation pearls? Not one of your friends will ever suspect it. You'll keep your fortune and possess a necklace which everyone will think is genuine. Isn't that lovely? Can't you just see yourself leading a full and happy life, with plenty of opportunity for fun and flirtation? Aha!" He waggled a jovial forefinger in her angry face.

At that moment Valérie had not the slightest desire for fun or flirtation. She glared at Jim Barnett with suppressed fury, and, drawing herself up, made her exit like a society queen withdrawing from a hostile drawing-room.

The little bag of pearls remained on the table.

"And they call that an honest woman!" said Jim Barnett to himself, his arms folded in virtuous indignation. "Her husband disinherits her to punish her for her naughty ways, and she disregards his wishes! There's a fresh will—and she filches it! She deceives his lawyer and despoils his old cousins. Tut, tut! And how noble is the part of the lover of justice who chastises the culprit and sets everything to rights again!"

He slipped the necklace deftly back into its place in the depths of his pocket, finished dressing, and then, his monocle carefully adjusted, and a fat cigar between his teeth, he left the office, and went forth in search of fresh amusement.

CHAPTER III

THE ROYAL LOVE LETTER

There was a knock at the door of the modest office in the *rue Laborde*.

It roused Jim Barnett of the Barnett Agency from his doze in the comfortable armchair, where he sat awaiting clients.

"Come in!" he cried, and, as the door opened to admit his visitor, "why, Inspector Béchoux, how nice of you to look me up! How are you?"

In both manner and appearance, Inspector Béchoux was a striking contrast to the usual type of detective. He aimed at sartorial elegance, exaggerated the crease in his trousers, had a pretty taste in ties and was very particular about the starching of his collars. He had a curious waxen pallor. In build, he was small, lean, and seemingly weedy. Oddly enough, he had the muscular arms of a heavyweight champion—arms which gave the impression of having been tacked haphazard on to his limp frame. He was intensely proud of those arms. Though quite a young man, his bearing was most self-assured. His eyes gleamed alert and intelligent.

"I happened to be passing," he announced, "and, knowing your clock-like habits, I thought: 'This being old Barnett's consultation hour, he's sure to be there. Why not drop in....'"

"And ask his advice," finished Jim Barnett.

"Perhaps," admitted the Inspector, to whom Barnett's perspicacity was a never-failing source of surprise.

Seeing his hesitation, Barnett spoke again: "What's up, old son? Finding it a bit difficult to consult the oracle to-day?"

Béchoux smote the table with his clenched fist; no mean blow, with his great arm to back it.

"Fact is, I'm a bit stumped. We've worked together on three cases now, Barnett—you as a private detective and I as a police inspector—and each time I haven't been able to help feeling that your clients—Baronne Assermann, for instance—ended by regarding you with a very jaundiced eye."

"As if I'd taken advantage of my opportunity to blackmail them," Barnett interrupted, fiddling with his eternal monocle, and smiling sardonically.

"No, I don't mean...." Béchoux forgot his resolve to find out just what *had* happened in the case of Baronne Assermann.

Barnett clapped him on the shoulder.

"Inspector Béchoux, you're forgetting the slogan of this firm: 'Information Free.' I give you my word of honor that I never ask my clients for a penny and I never accept a penny from them."

Béchoux breathed more freely.

"Thanks," he said. "I'm glad to have that assurance. My professional conscience will only allow me to avail myself of your coöperation on certain conditions. You understand, don't you? But if you don't mind my asking the question, there's one thing I feel I must know. Just what financial backing have you in the Barnett Agency?"

"I have a sleeping partner—a philanthropist." Barnett's tone was remote and casual.

"Is he anybody I know?"

"I rather think so. In fact, I'm almost certain. For even a police inspector must at some time have heard the name of—Arsène Lupin!"

Béchoux jumped.

"That's no name to jest about, Barnett."

Inspector Béchoux's existence was dominated by two emotions—his admiration for Barnett's detective ability and his fierce hatred of Arsène Lupin. Béchoux was one of Caminard's little band and fully shared that great man's bitterness, especially as he had himself suffered humiliating defeats at the enemy's hands. He still smarted with resentment at the memory of these, and never forgot that Arsène Lupin had added insult to injury by robbing him more than once of the lady of his choice.

"We won't discuss the fellow," he said gruffly, "unless there's a chance of my laying hands on him."

"Or I," and Barnett blandly extended his own hands—oddly enough, at the level of his nose! "But let's get to work. Whereabouts is your new job?"

"Near Marly. It's the business of the murder of old Vaucherel. You've heard about it?"

"Only vaguely."

Barnett's attitude was one of acute detachment from anything so mundane as murder.

"I'm not surprised. The newspapers aren't giving it much space yet, though it's infernally baffling...."

"He was done in with a knife, wasn't he?" After all, Barnett's detachment was only assumed.

"Yes. Stabbed between the shoulder-blades."

"Any finger-marks on the knife?"

"None. We found a piece of paper in ashes; it was probably wrapped round the handle by the murderer."

"Any clews?"

Inspector Béchoux shook his head. "Vaucherel's room was a bit disordered. Some of the furniture had been knocked over and the drawer of a table had been broken open, but we don't know why that was done or what's missing."

"Where have they got to on the inquest?"

"They're confronting a retired official called Leboc with the Gaudu cousins—three ne'er-do-weel blackguards of poachers. Without any real evidence, each side is accusing the other of the murder. Want me to run you over there in my car? Nothing like a good, stiff cross-examination, you know!"

"Right you are." Barnett rose, albeit reluctantly.

"Just one thing, Barnett. Formerie, who's conducting the inquiry, hopes to attract attention and get a Paris appointment. He's a touchy sort of chap and he won't stand for your usual bright bedside manner with the law, so cut out the flippancy." Béchoux's tone was eloquent with painful memories of Barnett's past exploits.

"I promise to treat him *most* respectfully," replied Barnett, "and I *never* break my word!"

Half-way between the village of Fontines and Marly Forest, in a copse separated from the forest by a strip of ground, stands a one-storied house with a small kitchen garden, surrounded by a low wall. Eight days before Béchoux's conversation with Jim Barnett, the cottage was still inhabited by a retired bookseller, old Vaucherel, who never left his little domain of flowers and vegetables except to browse in the bookstalls along the Paris quays. He was very miserly and reputed a rich man, although frugal in his habits. He had no visitors except his friend, Leboc, who lived at Fontines.

The reconstruction of the crime and the examination of Leboc were over, and the inspection of the garden had begun, when Jim Barnett and Inspector Béchoux alighted from their car. Béchoux made himself known to the gendarmes guarding the cottage gate and, followed by Barnett, he joined the examining magistrate and the deputy just as the latter had halted before an angle of the wall. The three Gaudu cousins were there to give their evidence. They were all three farm-hands of just about the same age; they bore no facial resemblance to one another save for a similar sly stubbornness of expression. The eldest Gaudu was speaking:

"Yes, your worship, that's where we jumped over when we ran to the rescue, as you might say."

"You were coming from Fontines?"

"Yes, your worship, from Fontines. We were on our way back to work, about two o'clock it must have been. It was like this: we were chatting with Mère Denise close by at the edge of the copse, when we heard screams. 'Somebody's crying for help,' I says. 'It's from the cottage.' Old Vaucherel, that we knew as well as anything, your worship. So we ran like mad. We climbed over this here wall—a nasty bit of work, with all them broken bottles on top—and we were across the garden in no time, as you might say."

"Where exactly were you when the front door flew open?"

"Right here," said the eldest Gaudu, leading the way to a flower-bed.

"That means about twenty yards from the porch," said the magistrate, pointing to the two steps leading up to the hall. "And from where you stood you saw——" He paused expectantly.

"Monsieur Leboc himself ... I saw him as clear as I see you, your worship ... he was rushing out, as if the devil was at his heels—or the police, for that matter, which they soon may be—and when he saw us he bolted straight back again."

"You're quite sure it was he?"

"I swear to God it was!"

The other two men took a similar oath.

"You can't have been mistaken?"

"Why, he's been living near our place for five years now, down the end of the village," the eldest Gaudu stated. "I've even delivered milk at his house!"

The magistrate gave an order. The door of the hall opened and a man came out. He was about sixty, and wore a brown drill suit and a straw hat. His face was pink and smiling.

The three Gaudus spoke simultaneously.

"Monsieur Leboc!"

Their choral affirmation made Leboc's entrance grotesquely like something in musical comedy.

The deputy whispered, "It's obvious there can't be any mistake at such close range and the Gaudu cousins can't have gone wrong on the identity of the fugitive—which means, of the murderer."

"Quite so," said the magistrate. "But are they speaking the truth? Was it Monsieur Leboc they saw? Now we'll go on."

The party went into the house and entered a big room whose walls were literally lined with books. There were just a few sticks of furniture; a large table—the one whose drawer had been broken into; and an unframed full-length portrait of old Vaucherel—a life-size daub by some unskilled artist who had yet managed to invest his subject with a certain verisimilitude.

A dummy lay stretched on the floor to represent the victim of the tragedy.

The magistrate resumed his examination.

"When you came on the scene, Gaudu, you did not see Monsieur Leboc again?"

"No, your worship. We heard groans from this room and rushed in at once."

"That means that Monsieur Vaucherel was still alive?"

"Hardly that, as you might say. He was lying face down with a knife stuck right in the middle of his back … we knelt down by him … the poor gentleman was trying to speak."

"Could you catch what he said?"

"No, your worship. We could only make out the name of Leboc—he said it over several times—'Monsieur Leboc, Monsieur Leboc …' like that. Then a kind of shudder passed over him and he was gone. After that we searched everywhere, but Monsieur Leboc had vanished. He must have jumped out of the kitchen window, which was open, and made off down the little gravel path. It goes straight to his house and the trees hide it all the way.… Then we all went together to the gendarmes … and we told them all about it.…"

The magistrate asked a few more questions, made the three cousins formulate even more definitely their charge against Monsieur Leboc, and then turned his attention to the latter.

Monsieur Leboc had listened without attempting to interrupt. His perfect calm was unruffled by any display of indignation. He gave the impression of finding the Gaudus' story so utterly absurd that he did not for a moment doubt that the magistrate would take a precisely similar view of it. Why bother to refute such a tale?

"Have you anything to add, Monsieur Leboc?"

"Nothing further."

"Then you still maintain——"

"I maintain what you, monsieur, know as well as I to be the truth. All the villagers you have examined have testified that I never go out during the daytime. At midday I have my lunch sent in from the inn. From one to four I sit at my window reading and smoking my pipe. The day in question was fine. My window was open, and five people—no less than five—saw me, as on any other day, from the garden gate."

"I have summoned them to appear later on."

"I'm glad to hear it. They will repeat their evidence. Since I am not ubiquitous and cannot at one and the same moment be here and in my own house you must admit that I could not have been seen leaving the cottage, that my poor friend Vaucherel could not have spoken my name in his agony, and therefore that these three Gaudus are unmitigated scoundrels."

"And you turn the murder charge against them, don't you?"

25

"Oh! Merely a matter of surmise...."

"On the other hand, an old woman, Mère Denise, who was out gathering firewood, states that she was talking with the men when they first heard the screams."

"She was talking with *two* of them. Where was the third?"

"A little way behind."

"Did she *see* him?"

"She thinks so ... she isn't positive...."

"In that case, what proof have you that the third Gaudu wasn't right here, committing the murder? What proof have you that the other two, posted near, didn't climb the wall, not to rush to the victim's help but to smother his cries and finish him off?"

"If that were so, why should they accuse you personally?"

"I have a small shoot and the Gaudus are incorrigible poachers. It was thanks to me that they were twice caught in the act and sentenced. Now, as they've got to accuse some one to shift suspicion from themselves, they're getting their own back."

"Merely surmise, as you said yourself. Why should they want to kill Vaucherel?"

"How should I know?" Leboc shrugged his shoulders.

"You have no idea what it was that may have been stolen from the drawer in the table?"

"None, your lordship. My friend Vaucherel was not rich, whatever people may have said. I happen to know that he had entrusted his savings to a broker and kept no money in the house."

"Nor anything valuable?"

"Nothing whatever."

"What about his books?"

"They aren't worth anything, as you can see for yourself. He always wanted to collect first editions and old bindings, but he could never afford it."

"Did he ever mention the Gaudu cousins to you?"

"Never. Much as I long to avenge my poor friend's death, I have no wish to speak anything but the strict truth."

The examination went on. The magistrate questioned the cousins closely, but at the finish the confrontation showed no results. Having cleared up a few minor points, the magistrates adjourned to Fontines.

Monsieur Leboc's property, at the end of the village, was no bigger than the cottage. The garden was enclosed by a very high, neatly clipped hedge. The white-painted brick house faced on to a tiny, perfectly circular lawn. As at the cottage the distance from gate to porch was between fifteen and twenty yards.

The magistrate asked Monsieur Leboc to take up his position as on the fatal afternoon. Monsieur Leboc thereupon seated himself at the window, a book on his knees, and his pipe in his mouth.

Here again no mistake was possible. Anyone passing the gate and glancing towards the house could not fail to see Monsieur Leboc distinctly. The five witnesses who had been summoned—laborers and shopkeepers of Fontines—repeated their evidence in such a way that it was quite impossible to doubt Monsieur Leboc's whereabouts between midday and four o'clock on the day of the crime.

The magistrates did not attempt to hide their bewilderment from the inspector, and Formerie, to whom Béchoux had introduced Barnett as a detective of exceptional ability, could not help saying:

"A complicated case, monsieur. What do you make of it?"

"Yes, what do you make of it?" echoed Béchoux, signing pointedly to remind Barnett of the need for tact.

Jim Barnett had followed the whole investigation at the cottage in silence. Béchoux had kept asking him questions, to which he had only replied with nods and muttered monosyllables. Now he answered pleasantly:

"A *most* complicated case, monsieur."

"Ah, you think so too. All things considered, the allegations of the two parties balance each other. On the one hand, we have Monsieur Leboc's alibi. It is incontestable that he could not have left his house that afternoon. On the other hand, the story of the three cousins impresses me favorably."

"That's so. One side or the other is acting an abject farce. But which side? Can the three Gaudus, bad characters of brutal aspect, be innocent? Or may the smiling Monsieur Leboc, all candor and calm, be guilty? Or are we to take it that the appearance of the actors in this drama is an indication of their respective rôles, Monsieur Leboc being innocent and the Gaudus guilty?"

"After all," Monsieur Formerie concluded with some satisfaction, "you're no nearer seeing daylight than we are."

"Oh, yes, I am!" Jim Barnett declared, a twinkle in his eye.

Monsieur Formerie bit his lip.

"That being so," he observed icily, "perhaps you will be so good as to tell us what more you have been able to discover."

"I will certainly do so at the proper moment. To-day, monsieur, all I can do is to beg you to call a new witness."

"A new witness? But—what's his name?"

"I really don't know."

"What's that? *You don't know?*"

Monsieur Formerie was wondering whether this super-detective was ragging him. Béchoux showed signs of anxiety. Was Barnett going to pull a

27

hornet's nest about his ears at the start?

At last Jim Barnett leaned over to Monsieur Formerie and pointing to Monsieur Leboc, who was still puffing conscientiously at his pipe by the window, he whispered:

"In the inner compartment of Monsieur Leboc's pocketbook there is a visiting card pierced with four small holes in lozenge formation. That card will give us the name and address of our new witness."

This ridiculous oracular pronouncement was hardly calculated to restore Formerie's equilibrium, but Inspector Béchoux did not hesitate to act. Without giving any reason, he ordered Monsieur Leboc to hand over his pocketbook. He opened it and took out a visiting card pierced with four holes arranged in a lozenge and bearing the name: *Miss Elizabeth Lovendale*, with an address in blue pencil: *Grand Hotel Vendôme, Paris*.

The two magistrates looked at one another in amazement. Béchoux fairly beamed, while Monsieur Leboc, utterly unembarrassed, exclaimed:

"Good gracious! What a search I had for that card! And so did poor Vaucherel!"

"Why should he have been looking for it?"

"Really, your lordship, you can't expect me to know that. I expect he wanted the address."

"Then what are the four holes doing?"

"Oh, I made those to mark the four points I scored in a game of *écarté*. We often played *écarté* together, and I must have picked this visiting card up without thinking and put it in my pocketbook."

Leboc gave this plausible explanation in a perfectly natural manner and it seemed to satisfy Formerie. What remained unexplained was how on earth Jim Barnett could have guessed that such a card was hidden in the pocketbook of a man he had never seen before in his life.

And Barnett himself furnished no elucidation. He merely smiled and insisted that they should call Elizabeth Lovendale as a witness. This they agreed to do.

Miss Lovendale was out of town and did not put in an appearance for a week. The inquiry was at a standstill for that time, although Formerie zealously pursued his investigations, the memory of Jim Barnett egging him on.

"You've riled him," Béchoux told Barnett on the afternoon when they were all assembled again at the cottage. "So much so that he's determined to decline your assistance."

"Ought I to clear out?" Barnett asked. "I don't want to cloud any one's sky—not even Formerie's!"

"No, you can stay," Béchoux told him. "Anyway, I fancy he's come to a definite decision."

"All the better. It's sure to be the wrong one. There's a good time coming!"

"Don't be so disrespectful, Barnett!"

"Oh, all right, I'll be respectful and, of course, absolutely disinterested. Nothing in hand or pocket. But, I must say, a little more Formerie will about finish me!"

Monsieur Leboc had been waiting half an hour when a car drew up and Miss Lovendale got out. Monsieur Formerie came up briskly.

"How do you do, Mr. Barnett," he said. "Any more bright ideas?"

"Perhaps, monsieur," was Barnett's cautious reply.

"Well, wait till you've heard mine. But first we must get through with your witness. Absolutely irrelevant and a sheer waste of time, you'll be glad to hear. Still, it can't be helped."

Elizabeth Lovendale was a dowdily dressed, middle-aged Englishwoman, her slight eccentricity of manner heightened by her dishevelled hair. She spoke French fluently, but so volubly that she was hard to understand.

At once, before any question could be put to her, she launched forth:

"That poor Monsieur Vaucherel! Murdered! Such a nice man, if he was a bit queer. And you want to know whether I knew him? Oh, not well. I only came here once—on business. I wanted to buy something from him. We disagreed about the price. I was going to have another appointment with him after seeing my brothers. My brothers are well known in London—Lovendale and Lovendale, Limited, the big provision merchants."

Monsieur Formerie strove to stem this flow of eloquence.

"What was it you wanted to buy, mademoiselle?"

"A little scrap of paper—nothing but a scrap of paper. Sentimental value only, as people say. But it was worth a lot to me and I made the mistake of telling him so. It all goes back to my great-grandmother, Dorothy Lovendale. She was a beauty and much admired by King George the Fourth. She kept eighteen love-letters that he wrote her and hid them, one in each volume of an eighteen-volume calf-bound edition of Richardson's works. When she died, the family found every volume except the fourteenth, which was missing, together with the letter inside of it—the fourteenth letter and the most interesting, for it was known to prove that the lovely Dorothy had stepped aside from virtue's path,"—Miss Lovendale lowered her eyes discreetly so as not to meet Barnett's look of amusement—"just nine months before the birth of her eldest son. You can understand what it would mean to us to get that letter back! Why, it would prove our royal descent!"

Formerie was growing more and more impatient.

Elizabeth Lovendale took a deep breath, and went on with her story.

"After searching and advertising for nearly thirty years, I learned one day that among a number of books sold at auction was the fourteenth volume of the set of Richardson. I flew to the purchaser, a second-hand bookseller on the *Quai Voltaire*, who referred me to Monsieur Vaucherel who had just bought the book. Monsieur Vaucherel produced the precious volume, and, like a fool, I told him that the letter I was after must be in the back of the binding. He examined it closely and changed color. Then, of course, I realized my stupidity. If I had kept quiet about the letter he would have sold me the book for fifty francs. I offered him a thousand. Monsieur Vaucherel, shaking with excitement, asked ten thousand. I agreed. We both lost our heads. It was like a nightmare auction. Twenty thousand—thirty—finally he demanded fifty thousand francs, yelling like a madman, with his eyes blazing. 'Fifty thousand,' he cried, 'not a sou less—that will buy me all the books I want—the rarest and finest—fifty thousand francs!' He wanted a deposit then and there—a check. I said I would come back. He let me go and I saw him lock the book into the drawer of this table."

Elizabeth Lovendale went on embellishing her statement with much unnecessary detail. Nobody paid any attention to her. All eyes were for the contorted countenance of the magistrate. He was obviously the prey of somewhat violent emotion and was quite overwhelmed with excessive jubilation. At last he managed to get out:

"In short, mademoiselle, you are asking for the return of the fourteenth volume of Richardson's collected works?"

"I am." She looked at him with sudden hope.

"Then here it is," he cried, and with a theatrical gesture he produced a small calf-bound book from his pocket.

"Not really!" cried Miss Lovendale.

"Here it is," he repeated. "But King George's love-letter isn't there. I should have noticed it. But I'll wager I can find it if I was able to discover the missing volume that people have been after for the past century. The man who stole the one indubitably stole the other."

Monsieur Formerie paced the room, his hands behind his back, enjoying his triumph. Suddenly he drummed on the table and spoke again.

"*Now* we know the motive for the murder. Someone overheard the conversation between Vaucherel and Miss Lovendale and saw where Vaucherel had put the book. A few days later that person murdered Vaucherel to rob him of the book so that he could later on dispose of the fourteenth letter. Who was it? Why, Gaudu, the farm-hand, whose guilt I never doubted. I searched his house yesterday and noticed a large crack between the bricks of the fireplace. Hidden in a hole behind this crack I found a book, which obviously belonged to Monsieur Vaucherel's library. Miss Lovendale's story, coming as it does, proves the accuracy of my deductions. The Gaudu cousins will be placed under arrest, the scum, as the murderers of poor old Vaucherel and the criminal accusers of Monsieur Leboc."

Monsieur Formerie solemnly shook hands with Monsieur Leboc as a mark of his esteem and was effusively thanked by the latter. Then he gallantly escorted Elizabeth Lovendale to her car and returned, rubbing his hands together.

After this, everybody made for the Gaudus' house, whither the three cousins were being brought under escort. It was a brilliant day. Monsieur Formerie, walking between Barnett and Béchoux, with Leboc bringing up the rear, was full of satisfaction. The coveted Paris appointment loomed ever nearer on his horizon.

"Well, well, Barnett," he remarked, "very neatly done, eh? Not quite what you expected, though. After all, you *were* inclined to be hostile to Monsieur Leboc, weren't you?"

"I admit, monsieur," Barnett confessed, "that I allowed my line of reasoning to be influenced by that confounded visiting card. Would you believe it? That card was lying on the cottage floor during the confrontation, and I actually saw Leboc drawing stealthily nearer and nearer till he got his right foot on it. When we left the place, he had it stuck to the sole of his boot. Afterwards he detached it and slipped it into his pocketbook. Well, the imprint of his right sole on the damp ground showed me that the said sole had four spikes arranged in a lozenge. That meant that our friend Leboc, knowing that he had forgotten the card lying on the floor, and anxious to keep Elizabeth Lovendale's name and address out of things, hit upon this neat little dodge. And really, it's thanks to the visiting card that——"

Monsieur Formerie burst out laughing.

"My dear Barnett, don't be childish! Why all these pointless complications? You shouldn't waste your energy ferreting out mares' nests. It's a thing I never do. For goodness sake let's stick to the facts as we find them and refrain from distorting them to fit impossible theories."

The party was by now near Monsieur Leboc's house which was on their way to the Gaudus'. Monsieur Formerie took Barnett's arm and went affably on with his curtain lecture.

"Where you went wrong, Barnett, was in refusing to admit the incontrovertible truth that, after all, one man cannot be in two places at the same moment. Everything turns on that—Monsieur Leboc, smoking at his window, couldn't be at the same time committing a murder at the cottage. Here we have Monsieur Leboc just behind us. There is the gate of his house, three yards away. I say it's impossible to conceive a miracle by which Monsieur Leboc could be at once behind us and at his window."

Suddenly Formerie stood still in his tracks, choking, helpless and amazed.

31

"What is it?" Béchoux asked.

Formerie pointed towards the house.

"There!... Look!..."

Through the bars of the gate, twenty yards away, beyond the lawn, they could see Monsieur Leboc smoking his pipe, framed in the open window—Monsieur Leboc who nevertheless was standing with the group in the road.

A nightmare vision—a hallucination! It was incredible. Who could be impersonating the real Leboc, whom Formerie had by the arm?

Béchoux had opened the gate and was running to the house. Formerie followed him, shouting threats at Leboc's extraordinary double. But the figure in the window never heeded nor stirred. How should it heed or stir, since, as they could see on drawing closer, it was merely a picture, a painted canvas fitting the window-frame exactly and presenting a tolerably life-like profile of Monsieur Leboc smoking his pipe. It was daubed in the same style as the portrait of Vaucherel hanging in the cottage. Obviously the same artist had painted both.

Formerie wheeled round. The mask of smiling placidity had dropped from Monsieur Leboc's face; the man had collapsed utterly under this unforeseen blow. He began a maudlin confession.

"I lost my head—I never meant to stab him—I only wanted to share in with him, fifty-fifty.... He refused—I didn't know what I was doing. I never meant to stab him."

His whining trailed off and Jim Barnett's voice, now harsh and scathing, was raised in mocking inquiry.

"What do you say to that, Monsieur Formerie? Nice lad, Leboc, all ready with a perfect alibi! How were the unobservant passers-by to doubt the reality of the Monsieur Leboc they only saw at a distance? Personally, I suspected something like this when I saw the portrait of old Vaucherel. I wondered if the same artist could have painted Leboc. I didn't have to look hard —Leboc was too sure he'd fooled us all. The canvas was rolled up and hidden in the corner of a shed under a heap of rusty tools. I only had to nail it in place at the window a little while ago, after Leboc had gone to answer your summons. That's how a man can simultaneously murder abroad and smoke his pipe at home!"

Jim Barnett was ruthless. His grating voice flayed the hapless Formerie.

"Just look what a clean sheet Leboc had. What a ready answer about the visiting card—the four holes marking his score at *écarté*. And the book he hid the other day in the Gaudus' fireplace. *I* was shadowing him! And the anonymous letter he sent you—for that was what got you going. Leboc, you scoundrel, I've had some real amusement out of you. D'you hear, my bright lad?"

32

Formerie was pale but restrained. After a prolonged scrutiny of Leboc, he murmured:

"I'm not surprised … shifty eyes … a slippery way with him.… What a rogue!" His wrath overflowed. "You blackguard, I'll see you get yours! Now then, where's that letter?"

Leboc, stricken helpless, stammered:

"In the bowl of the pipe that's hanging on the wall in the room on your left. I haven't cleaned it. The letter's there."

They rushed into the room. Béchoux fell upon the pipe and shook out the ashes. But the bowl was quite empty. Leboc seemed utterly overcome and Formerie's temper broke out again.

"You liar—you confounded faker! But you're going to tell me where that letter is—*at once*!"

At that moment the inspector met Barnett's gaze. Barnett was smiling a happy, childlike smile. Béchoux's fists clenched convulsively. He began to understand that the Barnett Agency was gratuitous in a peculiar fashion all its own. Dimly he saw how Jim Barnett, while protesting truthfully that he never asked his clients for a penny, could afford to live in comfort as a private detective.

He drew close to him and muttered:

"You think you're pretty clever, don't you? The Arsène Lupin touch!"

"What?" Barnett was all wide-eyed innocence.

"The way you spirited that letter away!"

"So you guessed my weakness? I always had a passion for the autographs of royalty!"

Three months later there called upon Elizabeth Lovendale, then in London, a highly distinguished gentleman, who assured her that he could lay hands on King George's love-letter to great-grandmother Dorothy. His price was a mere bagatelle of a hundred thousand francs.

There were lengthy negotiations. Elizabeth took counsel with her brothers, the renowned provision merchants. They haggled, refused to pay, and finally gave in.

The highly distinguished gentleman pocketed his hundred thousand francs and appropriated, into the bargain, an entire vanload of choice groceries which disappeared into the void!

CHAPTER IV

A GAME OF BACCARAT

Jim Barnett, making his way out of Rouen railway station, was met by Inspector Béchoux, who clutched his arm and led him quickly away.

"We haven't a minute to lose. Things may take a turn for the worse at any moment!"

"I should be much more impressed with the gravity of the situation," Barnett remarked with profound logic, "if I knew what it was all about. I came in answer to your wire and in complete ignorance of the excitements awaiting me."

"You arrived according to plan—*my* plan," said Inspector Béchoux complacently.

"Can this mean, Béchoux"—Barnett paused to strike a dramatic attitude —"can this mean that you've got over the little affair of King George the Fourth's love-letter and no longer distrust me?"

"I still distrust you, Barnett, just as I distrust the way the Barnett Agency settles accounts with its clients. But there's nothing in this case for you, old man. For once in your career you'll have to give your services gratis."

Barnett's lips pursed to a soft whistle. The prospect did not seem to daunt him. Béchoux gave him a swift sidelong glance, already uneasy and wishing that he could manage to dispense with the private detective's assistance.

They turned into the station yard. A private car was drawn up, waiting and in it sat a handsome woman with a pale, tragic face. Tears stood in her eyes and her lips were pressed together in a desperate effort at self-control. She opened the car door and Béchoux introduced his friend.

"Madame, this is Jim Barnett. I told you of him as the only man who might be able to save you. Barnett, let me introduce Madame Fougeraie— the wife of Monsieur Fougeraie, the engineer. Madame Fougeraie's husband is on the verge of being arrested on a charge of——" He paused dramatically.

"Of what?"

"Murder."

34

Jim Barnett's tongue clicked in ghoulish appreciation. The horrified Béchoux stammered an apology for his friend.

"Forgive him, madame. He always feels so utterly at home on a really serious case."

The car was already speeding towards the quays of Rouen. It turned left and drew up in front of a big building.

They all got out and went up in a lift to the third floor, on which were the premises of the Norman Club. "Here," said Béchoux waving a hand to indicate the palatial precincts, "is the rendezvous where the biggest merchants and manufacturers of Rouen and the district meet to talk, read the papers and play cards, especially on Friday, which is Stock Exchange day. As nobody is about in the morning except the cleaners, there is plenty of time for me to tell you on the spot about the drama that has just been enacted here."

They passed down a passage into a large, comfortably furnished room with a thick pile carpet. This, with two similar adjoining rooms, lined the façade of the third floor of the building. These rooms were intercommunicating, and the third led into a much smaller circular room, with only one window, opening on to a big balcony, which overlooked the banks of the Seine. They passed into the third large room.

There they all sat down, Madame Fougeraie a little withdrawn near a window, and Béchoux spoke:

"Now listen. A few weeks ago, on a Friday night, four members of this club sat down after a good dinner to play poker. They were all friends, mill-owners and manufacturers at Maromme, a big industrial centre near Rouen. Three of the men were married and the fathers of families: Alfred Auvard, Raoul Dupin, and Louis Batinet. The fourth, Maxime Tuillier, was a younger, unmarried man in the same set.

"Towards midnight a fifth member joined them—a rich, young idler, Paul Erstein by name. The five started playing baccarat now that the rooms were deserted. Paul Erstein, an enthusiastic and regular player, held the bank."

Béchoux pointed to one of the tables in the room, and went on:

"They were playing there, at that table. At first it was a quiet game—they had begun playing half-heartedly for want of something better to do—but gradually it warmed up, after Erstein had ordered two bottles of champagne for the party. From that moment luck was on the banker's side—shocking, unfair, maddening luck. Paul Erstein had it all his own way. The others were exasperated and did their utmost to break the run, without success. Contrary to all common sense, they would none of them give in, with the result that at four o'clock in the morning the Maromme manufacturers had lost all the money they were bringing from Rouen to pay their hands. In

35

addition, Maxime Tuillier had given Paul Erstein his I.O.U. for eighty thousand francs."

Inspector Béchoux drew a long breath and continued:

"Suddenly there was a *coup de théâtre*, a strange turn given to Fortune's wheel by Erstein's own happy-go-lucky generosity. He divided his winnings into four shares, corresponding exactly to the other men's losses, then subdivided those into thirds, and proposed having three final deals. This meant that each of his opponents was to play him individually double or quits on each of the three bundles of notes. They took him on. Paul Erstein lost all three deals. The luck had turned. After an all-night battle there were neither winners nor losers.

"'All the better,' said Erstein, standing up. 'I felt a bit ashamed of myself, winning like that. Lord! what a head I've got! Must be the heat of the room. Anyone coming to smoke a cigarette with me on the balcony?'

"He stepped into the Round Room. For a few minutes, the four friends remained at the table, gaily discussing the phases of the game. Then they decided to leave the club. After crossing the other two rooms, they warned the watchman dozing in the anteroom:

"'Monsieur Erstein is still there, Joseph. But he's sure to be going soon.'

"Then they left, at exactly thirty-five minutes past four. They went back to Maromme in Alfred Auvard's car, as on most Friday nights. The club servant, Joseph, waited for another hour. Then, tiring of his vigil, he went in search of Paul Erstein, and found him lying in the Round Room, twisted and inert. He was dead."

Inspector Béchoux paused again. Madame Fougeraie's head was bowed. Jim Barnett accompanied his friend into the Round Room, cast a searching glance over everything, and spoke:

"Now then, Béchoux, let's get down to it. What has the inquest revealed?"

"The inquest has revealed," answered Béchoux, "that Paul Erstein was struck on the left temple with a blunt instrument which must have felled him at a blow. There was no sign of a struggle except that his watch was broken. The hands pointed to five minutes to five, that's to say, twenty minutes after the departure of the other players. There was no indication of theft; a signet ring and a wad of notes had not been taken; nothing was missing. Finally, there was absolutely no trace of the murderer, who could not have come or gone by way of the anteroom, since Joseph had not moved from his post."

"Then," said Barnett, "there is no clue?"

"There is just one." Béchoux hesitated, then went on: "It's pretty important. At the inquest, one of my colleagues called the coroner's attention to the fact that the balcony on the third floor of the next building is very close to the balcony of this room. The magistrates entered the building in question, the third floor of which is the Fougeraies' flat. They found that Monsieur Fougeraie had left home that morning and had not returned. Madame Fougeraie took the magistrates into her husband's room. The balcony of that room is the one contiguous to the balcony of the Round Room. Look!"

Barnett stepped out through the open French window.

"The distance is about four feet," he observed. "Quite easy to get across. But there's nothing to prove that it was done."

"Wait a moment," said Béchoux. "D'you see those flower-boxes at the edge of the Fougeraies' balcony? They still contain the earth with which they were filled last summer. They've been searched. In one of them, just below the surface, with the earth freshly turned above it, we found a knuckle-duster. The coroner has established that the shape of this weapon corresponds exactly to the wound inflicted on Erstein. There were no finger-prints distinguishable, as it had been raining steadily since the morning. But the charge seems pretty well-founded. Monsieur Fougeraie, seeing Paul Erstein in the brilliantly lighted room opposite, must have sprung on to the club balcony; then, after murdering his victim with the knuckle-duster, he hid his weapon in the flower-box."

"But what motive had he for the crime? Did he know Paul Erstein?"

Béchoux shook his head.

"Then why——?"

During Béchoux's reconstruction of what had happened, Madam Fougeraie had got up and come over to where the two men stood. Her grief-stricken face worked pitifully. She kept back her tears with a visible effort. In answer to Barnett's question, she said in a voice that trembled:

"It is for me to answer, monsieur. I will be brief and perfectly frank, and then you will understand my fears. No, my husband did not know Paul Erstein. But *I* knew him. I had met him several times in Paris at a friend's house, and from the start he made love to me. I am devoted to my husband"—poor Madame Fougeraie gave a choking sob—"I have always been faithful to him. Although I was sensible of Paul Erstein's attraction, I resisted it. But, weakly, I gave in to the extent of meeting him several times in the country some way out of Rouen."

"And you wrote to him?"

She nodded miserably.

"And your letters are now in the hands of his family?"

"Of his father."

"Who, I suppose, is determined the letters shall be read in court so that his son's death shall be avenged at all costs."

"Yes. Those letters prove the harmless character of our relations. But—they prove that I met Paul Erstein without my husband's knowledge. And in one of them I wrote: 'I beg of you, Paul, do be reasonable. My husband is extremely jealous and very violent. If he should suspect me for an instant, he would be capable of doing almost anything.' So you see, monsieur, that letter would considerably strengthen the case against my husband. Jealousy would provide the police with the motive they want. It would explain the murder and the discovery of the weapon in the flower-box just outside my husband's room."

"Are you yourself sure, madame, that Monsieur Fougeraie suspected nothing?"

She nodded.

"And you believe him innocent?"

"Oh, there can be no doubt—no doubt at all!" she cried impulsively.

Barnett, meeting her steadfast gaze, realized how this woman's conviction of her husband's innocence could have influenced Béchoux to the extent of making him her ally despite the public prosecutor and his minions, and despite professional etiquette.

Barnett asked a few more questions, was lost in thought for some moments, and at last announced solemnly:

"Madame, I can hold out no hopes. Logically, your husband must be guilty. It is for me to try to disprove logic."

"Do see my husband," Madame Fougeraie besought him. "He will be able to explain——"

"That's quite useless, madame. I cannot help you unless I first of all put your husband right out of the running in my own mind, and work on the basis of your belief in his innocence."

The preliminaries were over. Barnett was in the ring at once, and, accompanied by Inspector Béchoux, called on the victim's father. With Erstein senior he came straight to the point:

"Monsieur, I am looking after Madame Fougeraie's interests for her. You are turning over your son's correspondence to the prosecution, aren't you?"

"To-day, monsieur."

"You have no hesitation in ruining the life of the woman your son loved so dearly?"

"If that woman's husband was my son's murderer, I shall be sorry for her sake, but my son's death shall be avenged."

"Wait five days, monsieur. Next Tuesday the murderer shall be unmasked."

Against his will, Erstein made the concession.

Barnett's procedure in those five days of grace often disconcerted Inspector Béchoux. He took—and made Béchoux take—the most irregular steps, interviewed and organized a band of helpers, and spent money like water. However, he seemed dissatisfied, and, contrary to habit, was taciturn and inclined to sulk.

On Tuesday morning he had a talk with Madame Fougeraie and told her:

"Béchoux has got the prosecution to agree to a reconstruction of the events of the fatal night, in detail, at the Norman Club, and it's to take place this afternoon. They have summoned both you and your husband to appear. I implore you to control yourself, whatever happens, and to try to appear almost indifferent."

She looked at him trustingly, through unshed tears.

"Is there any hope…?" she faltered.

"I don't know myself. As I told you before, I am simply playing your hunch that Monsieur Fougeraie is innocent. I shall try to prove his innocence by demonstrating a possible theory, but it's a difficult business. Even admitting that I am on the right track, as I believe I am, the truth may yet elude us up to the very last moment."

The public prosecutor and the examining magistrate who had investigated the case proved to be a conscientious pair. They put their trust in facts alone and refrained from interpreting these in the light of preconceived theories.

"With such men," said Béchoux, "I have no fear of your starting a row or employing your usual bright badinage. They have very kindly given me *carte blanche* to act as I see fit—or rather as *you* see fit—and don't you forget it."

"My dear Béchoux," replied Barnett, "I never indulge in badinage except when victory is within my grasp, which is not the case today."

The third room at the Norman Club was crowded. The magistrates talked together at the threshold of the Round Room; then they went into it, but came out again in a little while. The manufacturers waited in a group. Policemen and inspectors came and went. Both Paul Erstein's father and Joseph, the club servant, stood apart from the rest. Monsieur and Madame Fougeraie were together in a corner. He looked gloomy and preoccupied; she was even paler than usual. It was common knowledge now that the police had decided to arrest the engineer.

One of the magistrates addressed the four men who had played baccarat with Paul Erstein:

"Gentlemen, we are about to reconstruct what took place on the fatal Friday night. Will each of you please take up the position in which he sat at this table so that we have the game of baccarat exactly as it was played? Inspector Béchoux, you will hold the bank. Have you asked these gentlemen to bring exactly the same sums in notes as they had with them on the occasion in question?"

Béchoux nodded and sat down in the middle seat, with Alfred Auvard and Raoul Dupin on his left and Louis Batinet and Maxime Tuillier on his right. Six packs of cards were put out. The cards were cut to him and he shuffled.

Then an odd thing happened. Immediately, just as on that tragic night, luck favored the banker. With the same ease as Paul Erstein, Béchoux won. He won steadily, automatically, as it were, in an unbroken run, without any of the fluctuations and turns of fortune which had, after all, characterized the original game. This mechanical continuity gave the scene a strange, cinematographic quality. The game might have been a fantastic "quick motion" picture of what had originally taken place. The atmosphere of the proceedings began to tell on the players. Maxime Tuillier seemed ill at ease and twice made mistakes in his play. Jim Barnett grew irritated by the young man and at last officiously took his place at Béchoux's right hand.

Ten minutes later—for the film-like speed of the game accelerated unchecked—more than half the banknotes produced for the game by the four friends were stacked on the green cloth in front of Béchoux. Maxime Tuillier, as represented by Jim Barnett, began handing over I.O.U.'s.

The pace quickened again. The end of the game came soon. Suddenly Béchoux, as Paul Erstein had done, divided his winnings into four wads of notes, proportionate to the other men's losses, and subdivided each wad into three, thus leading up to Erstein's dramatic offer of "double or quits" on three deals.

His opponents' eyes never left him. The four men were evidently stricken by the memory of that other game.

Three times Béchoux dealt on the two *tableaux*.

And three times, instead of losing, like Paul Erstein, Béchoux won!

A murmur of surprise rose from the onlookers. The miraculous reconstruction of the original game had been unaccountably flawed. The luck should have turned—but it had remained in the banker's favor. Supposing —the thought slipped into being—supposing this was indeed a miracle, and this new ending to the game was *not new at all*?

"I am sorry," said Béchoux, his words oddly remote as he continued to act his rôle of banker. He stood up, first pocketing all the banknotes.

Then, as Paul Erstein had done, he complained of a headache and expressed his wish that someone would come out on the balcony with him. He went out, lighting a cigarette.

The other men remained motionless, with set faces. The cards lay scattered on the table.

Then, and only then, Jim Barnett rose from his chair. But now, by some wizardry, his face and his general appearance had taken on the outward semblance of Maxime Tuillier, whom he had so lately supplanted in the game of baccarat. Maxime Tuillier, clean-shaven, about thirty, wearing a tight-fitting, double-breasted coat.... Maxime Tuillier, looking morose and dissatisfied.... Jim Barnett was the young man to the life!

He went slowly towards the Round Room, moving like an automaton, his expression an alternating study in callous ruthlessness and frightened indecision—the expression of a man on the verge of doing something terrible, but a man who might yet perhaps take to his heels with the deed unaccomplished.

The players could not see his face, which was turned away from them. But the magistrates saw it. And they forgot Jim Barnett, the skilled impersonator, and thought only of Maxime Tuillier, the ruined gambler, who was going to join his triumphant opponent. His face, which he apparently strove to compose, gave ample indication of his mental turmoil. Was he about to make a plea, a demand, or—a threat? When he opened the door of the Round Room, he was once more master of his emotions; he had regained his self-control.

The door closed behind him.

The staging of the imaginary "reconstruction" of the drama had been so vivid that everyone waited in silence. The other players also waited, staring at that closed door behind which was being repeated what had taken place on the night of the tragedy—behind which it was not Barnett and Béchoux who were playing their respective rôles of murderer and victim, but Maxime Tuillier and Paul Erstein pitted against one another.

After what seemed an eternity, the murderer—there was nothing else to call him—came out. He staggered back to his friends, his eyes wild with horror. In one hand he held the four bundles of notes. One he threw down on the table. The other three he pressed upon the three players, saying in queer, strained tones:

"I've been having a talk with Erstein. He asked me to give you back this money. He doesn't want it. Let's go home."

A yard or so away Maxime Tuillier, the real Maxime Tuillier, leaned on a chair for support. His face was pale and drawn. His jaw had fallen. Jim Barnett turned and spoke to him in his normal voice.

"Am I right, Monsieur Tuillier? The scene has been reproduced correctly in all essential details, hasn't it? My rendering of the part you played the other night was pretty accurate? Don't you think I've reconstructed the crime rather cleverly—*your* crime?"

Maxime Tuillier seemed not to hear the words. His head was bowed; his arms hung limp. He was a mere husk of a man, all the life gone out of him. He reeled drunkenly, sagged at the knees, and collapsed on the chair.

Barnett was at him at once, jerking him roughly to his feet.

"You admit it? But anyway, nothing can save you. I can prove everything. First, that knuckle-duster—you always carried one. Then, you were ruined by your losses at baccarat that night. Investigations have established the fact that you were in financial straits. You had no money with which to meet your creditors at the end of the month. You were on the verge of bankruptcy. When you followed Erstein into the Round Room, you struck out, murderously. Afterwards, not knowing what to do with your weapon, you climbed over on to the other balcony and hid it in the flower-box. Then you altered the hands of the dead man's watch to establish your alibi, and joined your friends!"

But Barnett's eloquent denunciation was unnecessary. Maxime Tuillier made no attempt at denial. Overwhelmed by the terrible burden of crime under which he had labored for weeks, he stammered out the confession of his guilt like a man in delirium.

The onlookers were roused almost to frenzy. The examining magistrates bent over the murderer and took down his involuntary, unprompted confession. Paul Erstein's father tried to hurl himself upon his son's slayer. Fougeraie's voice was raised excitedly. But the most rabid were Maxime Tuillier's three friends. One in particular, the eldest and most influential, Alfred Auvard, volleyed abuse:

"You unspeakable blackguard! You made us believe that poor Erstein had returned the money to us—when really you had stolen it after murdering him!"

He flung the notes at Maxime Tuillier's head. The other two, equally indignant, trampled the loathsome money underfoot.

By degrees order was restored. Maxime Tuillier, half fainting and uttering groans, was carried out of the room. An inspector gathered up the banknotes and handed them to the magistrates. The latter requested the Fougeraies and old Erstein to withdraw. They then complimented Jim Barnett on his extraordinary powers of deduction.

"Tuillier's collapse and confession," he told them, "are quite commonplace features in the case. Its originality, the *real* mystery that lifts it out of the usual run of such crimes, lies in something quite different. So now, although this is none of my business, please allow me——"

Barnett, turning to the three manufacturers who were talking together in low tones, went up to them and tapped Monsieur Auvard gently on the shoulder.

"A word with you, my friend. Something tells me you can throw a little light on one aspect of this case that remains obscure."

"In what connection, pray?" asked Auvard coldly.

"In connection with the part which you and your friends play in it, monsieur."

"But we don't come into it at all!"

"Not actively, of course, I quite see that. But there are some features which, I am sure you will agree with me, present a disconcerting series of contradictions. For instance, you declared on the morning after the murder that the game of baccarat had ended with three deals *in your favor*, which cancelled your losses and broke up the card party. Well, the facts don't happen to bear out your statement."

Monsieur Auvard answered him defiantly:

"That's so. But there's been a misunderstanding. Actually, those last three deals only increased our losses. When Erstein left the table, Maxime, who seemed perfectly self-possessed, followed him into the Round Room for a smoke, while we three remained here, talking. When Tuillier came back, nearly ten minutes later, he told us that Erstein had never been in earnest over the game, that it had merely been a series of flukes following on the champagne, to be treated as a joke. He therefore insisted on returning the money to us, but pledged us to secrecy. If anything ever came out, we were to say that the end of the game had evened things up unexpectedly."

"And you accepted such an offer! As a present from Paul Erstein which he had absolutely no reason to make you!" cried Barnett. "And having accepted it, you didn't even bother to thank him! And you found it perfectly natural that Erstein, who was an inveterate gambler, inured to gain and loss alike, should suddenly be ashamed to profit by his luck! *How* unlikely!"

"It was four in the morning. We were all overwrought. Maxime Tuillier gave us no time for reflection. Anyhow, what reason had we to doubt his word? We didn't know then that he had just murdered Erstein and robbed him."

"But next day you learned of the murder."

"Yes, but we naturally thought it had happened after our departure from the club—it made no difference to Erstein's last action on earth—the restoration of our losses—nor to his wish that we should hold our tongues about it."

"And you never for one moment suspected Maxime Tuillier?"

"Why should we have suspected him? He is a member of the club. His father was a friend of mine and I've known him practically all his life. Of course we had no suspicions."

"Are you positive?"

Barnett rapped the words out in ironic incredulity. Alfred Auvard hesitated, glanced at the other two men, and then countered haughtily:

"Your questions, sir, are in the nature of a cross-examination. What do you think we're here for anyway?"

"In the eyes of the law you're here as witnesses. But in mine——"

"In yours——?"

"That's just what I'm going to explain now." Quietly Barnett took the floor, toying with the string of his monocle.

"The whole of this case is really dominated by one factor—the confidence you people inspired. Practically speaking, the crime could have been an outside or an inside job. Yet those investigating at once turned to the outside for the simple reason that one does not normally suspect such a monument of respectability and righteousness as is constituted by four wealthy manufacturers of unblemished reputation. If *one* of you, say, Maxime Tuillier, had played a game of *écarté* with Paul Erstein *alone*, he would naturally and undoubtedly have been suspected. But there *were* four of you, and Tuillier was temporarily saved by the silence of his friends. It would never occur to anyone that three men of your standing could be guilty of complicity in a crime! Yet you *were* guilty—and that was what I guessed from the start."

Alfred Auvard started forward.

"You must be mad. Do you seriously suggest that we were Tuillier's accomplices?"

"Oh, no. Obviously, you had no idea of what was going on in the Round Room after Tuillier joined Erstein there. But you *did* know that he had followed him in a peculiar frame of mind! And when he came back, you knew that *something* had happened."

"We knew nothing of the sort."

"Oh, yes, you did, and that Tuillier must have used force of some kind. There had not necessarily been a crime of violence, but there had certainly not been merely a friendly conversation. I repeat, it was quite evident that Maxime Tuillier must have used force to get back that money for you."

"Preposterous!"

"Not at all. When a coward like your friend kills a man, his face is bound to betray him. It is impossible that you should have utterly failed to notice his expression of horror when he came back after committing the crime."

Both Batinet and Dupin were trembling, but Auvard kept up his blustering attitude.

"I protest that we noticed nothing."

"None so blind...." Barnett shrugged his shoulders and smiled unpleasantly.

"What do you mean by that?"

"You didn't *want* to see. Because you had got your money back. I know you are all rich men. But that game of baccarat had shaken you considerably. Like all occasional gamblers, you had the feeling that your money had been stolen from you, and when it was returned, you accepted it without troubling to inquire too closely into the methods by which your friend had recovered it. You clung desperately to silence. That night, as you drove back to Maromme together, in spite of the urgent need for you to agree upon a safer version of the evening's episode, not one of you dared speak a word. I have that from your chauffeur. And the next day—and the days after that—when the crime had been discovered, you avoided meeting each other, for fear of finding your secret thoughts confirmed."

"This is mere conjecture." Auvard was indignant still, but his two friends were on the verge of collapse.

"Not conjecture, but certainty," Barnett corrected him gently. "Certainty based on facts acquired by exhaustive inquiries among the people who know you. For you to accuse your friend was to expose your own criminal weakness in the beginning. It meant turning the searchlight of public opinion on yourselves and your families, and damaging your reputations for honorable dealing with your fellow-men. It meant a scandal. So you kept silent and cheated justice while you shielded your friend Maxime."

Jim Barnett had been so vehement and telling in his accusation that for a moment Monsieur Auvard wavered. But, suddenly changing his tactics, the bewildering Barnett did not follow up his advantage. He merely laughed and said:

"Cheer up, Monsieur Auvard. I succeeded in undoing your friend Tuillier because he was a weakling and suffering the agonies of remorse. I did it by faking the cards in the game of baccarat we had here just now. The accuracy of the reconstruction unnerved him. But I had no more *real* proof against him than I have against you, and you are not the sort to give in without showing fight. All the more so as your complicity in the crime is so vague and negative, very much up in the air when it comes to hard facts. So you have nothing to fear. Only"—he came closer to his man, and thrust his face into the other's—"only, I did not want your peace of mind to be too complete. By your silence and your astuteness, the three of you managed to cloak your actions from the light of the law, so that people lost sight of your own more or less voluntary complicity in the crime. We can't have that, though. You must never cease to be conscious that to a certain extent you shared in the committal of the murder. Had you only prevented your friend from following Paul Erstein into the Round Room, as you should have done, Paul Erstein would not be dead today. And had you come forward at the outset and told what you knew, Maxime Tuillier would not have come within an ace of escaping his deserts.

"Now it is for you to clear yourselves as best you may, messieurs. Somehow, I don't think the law will be too hard on you. Good-day."

Jim Barnett took his hat, and, disregarding the manufacturers' protest, spoke to the magistrates:

"Messieurs, I promised Madame Fougeraie that I would help her and I promised Paul Erstein's father to unmask the murderer. My work is done."

The magistrates were half-hearted in their valedictory handshake. Probably Barnett's words had fallen none too pleasantly on their ears and they did not feel particularly inclined to follow his lead.

To Inspector Béchoux, who had followed him on to the landing, Barnett was just a wee bit more expansive:

"Those three chaps can't be touched. They're safe as houses. Blasted bourgeois bolstered up by bullion!" he almost blew bubbles in his wrath. "They're pillars of society, all right, and all the case against them is the inferences to be drawn from my deductions. Too fine a thread for the law to noose them in, I'm afraid. Never mind, I've brought my case off well."

"*And* honestly," approved Béchoux, adding, *sotto voce*, the words "for once!"

Barnett's eyebrows arched interrogatively.

"I must own," Béchoux admitted, "that there were moments when I feared for those banknotes. You could have snaffled them so easily."

"What *do* you take me for, Inspector Béchoux? A common thief?" Barnett's tone was one of outraged innocence.

He left his friend and went out of the building and on to the Fougeraies' flat next door. There he was effusively thanked. With great dignity he refused to take any reward for his services.

Afterwards he called on Paul Erstein's father and there exhibited the same spirit of disinterested philanthropy.

"The services of the Barnett Agency are free," he told his clients. "That is the secret both of its efficiency and of its integrity. We work for glory only."

Jim Barnett settled his hotel bill and ordered them to send his bag to the station. Then, presuming that Béchoux would accompany him back to Paris, he walked along the quayside to the club building. On the first landing he halted abruptly. The inspector was hurtling down the stairs. The moment he saw Barnett he cried out angrily:

"Got you, curse you!"

He jumped the remaining stairs at a bound and thrust his fingers inside Barnett's coat collar.

"What have you done with those notes?"

"Doh, ray, me, fah——" began Barnett.

"*Banknotes!*" the inspector screamed. "The notes you had when you were acting Tuillier's part upstairs."

"What's all this? Do let go my collar. That's better. Why, I gave those notes back. Surely you remember? A little while ago you were even congratulating me on my honesty!"

"I wouldn't have if I'd known what I know now!" said Béchoux grimly.

"And what is this new knowledge that makes you change your tune?" chanted Barnett.

"The notes you gave back are forgeries—counterfeit—snide!" Béchoux was frothing at the mouth. "You're a rotten swindler!" he shouted. "You needn't think you're going to get away with it, either. You're going to return the genuine notes to me *at once*! You can't bluff *me*!"

He choked, and Barnett's raucous laugh rent the air.

"The thieving skunks!" he exclaimed. "Well, well, well. So they threw forged notes at their young friend. The sweeps! We get them to bring their wads along and they turn out to be stage money!"

"But don't you understand?" Béchoux shrieked dancing with rage. "That money belongs to Paul Erstein's heirs. He had won it before he was killed. The others must make restitution."

Barnett's merriment overflowed.

"Isn't that too bad! So they're to be fleeced twice over. Poetic justice being visited on the scoundrels!"

Béchoux's teeth chattered with fury.

"You liar! You changed those notes yourself. And now you've collared the cash. Thief! Crook!"

As the magistrates were leaving the club they caught sight of Inspector Béchoux gesticulating speechlessly, frantically. And before him, arms folded, convulsed with laughter, there leant against the wall—"Jim Barnett!"

CHAPTER V

THE MAN WITH THE GOLD TEETH

Jim Barnett held back a corner of his office window-curtain and peered into the street, his face on a level with those of the passers-by. Suddenly he was seized with a paroxysm of uncontrollable mirth and sank weakly back into his armchair.

"Almost too beautiful," he murmured ecstatically.

"To think the day should come when Béchoux——" He subsided into fresh guffaws.

"What's the joke?" was Inspector Béchoux's immediate demand on entering the office.

As Barnett did not at once reply, he fixed him with a stony glare.

"What—are—you—laughing at?"

"Why, at your coming here, of course! After our dust-up at the club in Rouen you actually feel you can seek me out again! What is our police force coming to?"

Béchoux looked so crestfallen that Barnett made a valiant effort to restrain his own unseemly laughter. But he could not control himself completely and his utterance continued to be punctuated by explosive chuckles.

"Awfully sorry, old chap, but it really *is* funny! You, the instrument of the law, presenting me with yet another pigeon for my plucking. Who is it this time? Dare I hope for a millionaire? Or am I in for the Minister of Finance? Don't mind me. I'm not particular. Really, though, it's frightfully decent of you, old chap! Pardon my familiarity. Cheer up, now, and try not to look like a decayed zebra. Spit it out!" (Barnett's idiom was deplorably vulgar.) "What's up? Someone in trouble again?"

Béchoux, struggling to regain his composure, nodded his head.

"Yes. It's the very worthy *curé* of a parish in the suburbs."

Regardless of grammar, "Who's he killed?" asked Barnett with interest. "One of his flock?"

"Oh, no, not *that*!"

"You mean *he's* been polished off by a parishioner? Then, really, I fail to see how I can assist him!"

"No, no. You're getting it all wrong. I—he——"

"I really think," said Barnett kindly, "you'd do better not to attempt to talk at all. You can't apparently achieve coherence, and I hate people who splutter in my face." He made great play with a virulent bandana. "Without further ado, lead me to your worthy suburban *curé*. I am ever ready to hit the trail with Béchoux for my guide."

The little village—it is no more—of Vaneuil straggles down a hollow and then up the three green hillsides which frame its old Romance church. Behind the church lies a tranquil country graveyard, which is bordered on the right by the hedge of a large estate surrounding a big farmhouse, and on the left by the wall of the rectory.

Béchoux, accompanied by Barnett, entered the latter building, walked straight into the dining-room and there presented his friend to the Abbé Dessole. He introduced Barnett as the one detective whose bright lexicon knew not the word "impossible."

The abbé certainly appeared to be a worthy—and probably a simple—man. He was middle-aged, plump, pink, and unctuous. His anxiety was written large on a face that must usually have worn an expression of unruffled placidity. Barnett observed his rather puffy hands, the rolls of fat at wrist and neck, the fat paunch distending the cheap, shiny cassock.

"Père Dessole," said Barnett, "I know nothing about whatever it is that troubles you. My friend, Inspector Béchoux, has so far merely told me that he first made your acquaintance a long while ago. Could you now give me a brief résumé of the facts of the case, avoiding all irrelevant detail?"

The Abbé Dessole must have prepared his story, for immediately, without a moment's hesitation, his deep bass voice boomed from the depths of his double-chin and he began:

"First, monsieur, I must tell you that the humble priests officiating in this parish act at the same time as custodians of a church treasure—the bequest in the eighteenth century of the lords of the Château Vaneuil.

"This treasure included two gold monstrances, two crucifixes, some candelabra, and a tabernacle, making in all—or, rather, as I must unfortunately say, which *made* in all nine valuable pieces which people even came here from a distance to see. Personally"—the Abbé Dessole mopped his brow and resumed: "Personally I must say that I always felt the custody of this treasure to be a perilous trust, and in fear and trembling I exercised every possible care in the discharge of my duty. From this window you can see the apse of the church, and the vestry where the treasure was kept. The walls of the vestry are exceptionally thick, and it has just the one great oak door opening into the chancel. I am the only person with a key to it, and that key is enormous. In addition to that, I am the possessor of the only existing key to the chest in which the treasure was locked. No one but myself ever acted as cicerone to the visitors who came to see the treasure."

He waggled a fat forefinger at Barnett and his tone took on added weight.

"My bedroom window, monsieur, is less than fifteen yards away from the barred dormer window which lights the vestry from above. Unknown to a soul, I used, every night, to stretch a rope from my room to the vestry so that any attempt at burglary would ring a bell at my bedside. As an additional precaution, I always took the most precious piece in the collection—a gem-studded reliquary—to my own room. Well, last night——"

The Abbé Dessole again mopped his brow. The sweat poured off him as he continued the unfolding of the tragedy.

"Last night, towards one o'clock, I sprang out of bed, staggering in the dark and only half-awake. I had been roused, not by the ringing of my bell, but by a noise which might have been caused by something being dropped on the floor. I called out:

"'Who's there?'

"There was no reply, but I could feel the presence of someone standing quite close to me, and I was sure the intruder had climbed in at the window, for I felt the night air blowing in. I groped for my flashlight, found it, and switched it on. Then, just for a second, I had a glimpse of a distorted face showing white between a grey slouch hat and a brown, turned-up collar. And in the man's mouth, which was moving silently, I could distinctly see two gold teeth, on the left side of the jaw."

A flicker of interest crossed Barnett's face.

"The man at once struck my arm a sharp blow so that I dropped the flashlight.... I rushed forward, but—he wasn't there! It was just as if I myself had spun round before moving, for I bumped into the mantelpiece over my fireplace, which is exactly opposite the window. By the time I had managed to find matches and strike a light there was no one in the room. A ladder had been left propped against the ledge of the balcony—one of my own ladders taken out of the shed. I got into some clothes and ran to the vestry. The treasure was gone!"

For the third time the abbé wiped his streaming countenance. He was pitifully moved.

"Of course," said Barnett, "you found the dormer window broken and your bell-rope cut through? Which proves, doesn't it, that the thief was someone familiar with this place and with your habits? And after your discovery you were on his track at once?"

"I even yelled 'Thief!' which was a mistake on my part, as it was the sort of thing to rouse the neighborhood and create a sensation. And heaven knows," he said gloomily, "this affair is bound to make a stir for which I shall be blamed by my superiors. Luckily, the only person who heard my shouting was my neighbor, Baron de Gravières. He has lived next door to me for twenty years now, engaged in the personal management of his estate. He absolutely agreed with me that, before notifying the police and lodging a formal complaint, it was advisable to try to recover the stolen property. As he has a car, I asked him to motor to Paris and bring back Inspector Béchoux."

"And I was on the spot by eight in the morning," said Béchoux, swelling with pride. "By eleven I had my case."

"What's that?" ejaculated Barnett in surprise. "You've caught the thief?"

Béchoux pointed pompously to the ceiling, rather in the manner of one indicating the path to paradise.

"He's up there, locked in the attic, and Baron de Gravières is mounting guard."

"Fine! A masterpiece of detection! Tell me all, Béchoux, but in tabloid form, since life is brief."

"A bare statement of facts will suffice," said the inspector, whose speech could achieve almost telegraphic condensation in the moment of victory: "(*a*) I found numerous footprints on the damp ground between the church and the vicarage; (*b*) An examination of said footprints proved that there was only one burglar, who first carried his haul from the vestry some distance away, since he returned to the attack by the vicarage steps; (*c*) The burglar, having waked Père Dessole, hurriedly retraced his steps, collected his loot and fled along the highroad. His tracks vanished near the Hippolyte Inn."

"Immediately," interrupted Barnett, "you cross-examined the innkeeper...."

"And the innkeeper," continued Béchoux, "on my inquiring for a man with a grey hat, a brown overcoat, and two gold teeth, told me at once that the description exactly fitted a certain Monsieur Vernisson. This man, he said, was a traveller in pins, known in Vaneuil as Monsieur Quatre-Mars, because he was in the habit of coming each year on the Fourth of March. The innkeeper told me that he had got in the day before at midday, had stabled his gig, eaten his lunch, and then gone off to call on his customers. I asked when he had got back, and the innkeeper told me about two in the morning, as usual. After that, I ascertained that the man in question had only been gone forty minutes and was driving in the direction of Chantilly."

"Whereupon," said Barnett, "you followed in his train?"

"The baron drove me in his car. We soon caught up with friend Vernisson and, though he protested, we forced him to put his gig about and come along with us."

"Ah, then he maintains his innocence?"

51

"Scarcely that. But all we can get out of him is 'Don't tell my wife!…
My wife must never learn of this!'"

"What about the treasure?"

The abbé sighed dolorously and Béchoux's triumph grew less pronounced.

"It wasn't in the gig."

"But you nevertheless find the evidence quite conclusive?"

"Oh, absolutely. Vernisson's shoes correspond exactly to the footprints
in the graveyard. Besides, the *curé* can swear to having encountered the
man there late that afternoon. There can be no doubt at all."

"Well then," said Barnett a trifle impatiently, "what's bothering you?
Why call *me* in?"

"Oh, that's an idea of the *curé's*," said Béchoux, looking a bit disgrun-
tled. "There's a minor point in the case on which we disagree."

"Minor! That's only in your opinion," said the Abbé Dessole, whose
handkerchief was by now wringing wet.

"What's the trouble, father?" asked Barnett.

"Well," the priest hesitated. "It's about——"

"Yes?" encouraged Barnett.

"About those gold teeth. Monsieur Vernisson certainly *has* two gold
teeth, only"—he faltered—"only, they're on the *right* side of his mouth …
whereas those *I saw* were on the *left*!"

Jim Barnett could not restrain his hilarity. He burst into loud laughter. As
the Abbé Dessole stared at him in blank amaze, he pulled himself together
and exclaimed:

"On the right side! Too bad! But are you sure you weren't mistaken?"

"Positive!"

"But you had met the man——"

"In the graveyard. Yes, that was Vernisson. But it couldn't have been the
same man who came in the night, since Vernisson's gold teeth are on the
right side, and the burglar's were on the left."

"Perhaps he had changed them over to make it more difficult," Barnett
suggested joyously. "Béchoux, do bring in the prisoner."

Two minutes later Monsieur Vernisson was ushered in. He was forlorn
and crushed looking, his melancholy aspect intensified by the depressed
droop of his moustache. His escort, Baron de Gravières, was a well set-up
specimen of the gentleman-farmer class, and carried a revolver. The prisoner, who looked dazed began moaning:

"I don't understand … a broken lock … what does it all mean?"

"You'd better confess," advised Béchoux, "instead of whining like that."

"I'll confess anything you like, if only you'll promise not to tell my
wife. That I can't allow. I have to meet her next week at Arras. I must be

there, and I can't have her know anything of this."

He was so frightened and upset that in his distress his mouth fell open and the gleam of the two gold teeth was apparent. Jim Barnett came up to him, inserted thumb and forefinger, and pronounced gravely:

"They're not a bit loose. There's no getting away from it, this chap's teeth are on the right side. And here's Père Dessole saying he saw them on the left."

Inspector Béchoux was livid.

"That makes no difference! We've caught the thief. He's been coming to the village for years preparing the ground for this robbery. The thing's as clear as day. The *curé* must be wrong!"

The Abbé Dessole solemnly extended his arm.

"I call upon God to witness that I saw the teeth on the left!"

"On the right!"

"On the left!"

"Time!" cried Barnett. "Now then, you two, you won't get anywhere with this 'Katy Did' business. What is it you're after, father?"

"A satisfactory explanation."

"And if you don't get it?"

"Then I shall turn the case over to the police as I ought to have done in the beginning. If this man is not guilty, we have no right to detain him. I maintain that the burglar's gold teeth were on the left side of his mouth."

"Right!" bawled Béchoux.

"Left!" the abbé insisted.

"Neither right nor left," was Barnett's dictum. He was in his element. "Father, I promise you to produce the thief here, tomorrow morning at nine, and he will tell you himself where to find the treasure. You, Béchoux, shall spend the night in this armchair, the baron in that one and we will tie Monsieur Vernisson to this one. Béchoux, will you wake me at a quarter to nine? I drink chocolate with my breakfast. See that there's toast—and I like my eggs lightly boiled."

By the end of that day, Barnett had been seen all over the place. He was seen making a minute examination of each tombstone in the graveyard in turn. He was seen searching the *curé's* bedroom. He was seen telephoning from the post-office. He was seen at the Hippolyte Inn, where he dined with the proprietor. He was seen striding along the highroad and strolling in the fields. But those who observed his actions could only guess at their purport.

He did not return until two o'clock next morning. The baron and the inspector were sitting very close to the man with the gold teeth, their snores reverberating in competitive crescendo. When he heard Barnett come in, Monsieur Vernisson groaned.

"Mustn't let my wife get to know of this...."

Jim Barnett flung himself down on the floor and was fast asleep at once.

At a quarter to nine precisely Béchoux woke Barnett. Breakfast was ready. Barnett wolfed four bits of toast, three cups of chocolate, and a couple of eggs. Then he invited his audience to gather round and said:

"Father, behold me punctual to the appointed hour. Now, Béchoux, I'm going to demonstrate the extreme unimportance of all your professional sleuth stuff—footprints, and cigarette ends, and so forth—when confronted with the actual facts of the case as reconstructed by an alert intelligence, spurred by intuition and ballasted with experience." He bowed modestly, seemingly unconscious that he was a trifle mixed in his metaphors. "We'll begin with Monsieur Vernisson."

"Anything—you can do anything—so long as you don't tell my wife," stammered the wretched commercial traveller, a wreck from anxiety and insomnia.

So Jim Barnett launched forth.

"Eighteen years ago Alexandre Vernisson, who was then already a traveller in pins, met here, in Vaneuil, a girl called Angélique, the little dressmaker of the village. It was a case of love at first sight on both sides. Monsieur Vernisson got several weeks' leave from his employers. He courted Mademoiselle Angélique, and they eloped. She loved him dearly and was his devoted companion until her death, two years later. He was quite inconsolable, and although later on a forward young woman called Honorine got him to marry her, his memories of Mademoiselle glowed the brighter, since Honorine, a jealous shrew, never ceased nagging at him and reproaching him with his two years' idyll, which had somehow come to her knowledge. Hence the pathetic pilgrimage in secret to Vaneuil which Alexandre Vernisson has made without fail each year. That's so, isn't it, Monsieur Vernisson?"

"Have it your own way," muttered the latter, "only don't tell...."

Jim Barnett went on:

"So, each year, Monsieur Vernisson plans his rounds so as to call at Vaneuil in his gig, unknown to Madame Honorine. He kneels beside the tomb of Angélique on each anniversary of her death, for it was here in this graveyard she was buried according to her dying wish. He revisits the places where they walked together on the day they first met, and returns to the inn at two in the morning, just as on that occasion. Not far from where we are sitting at this moment you can see the humble headstone with the inscription that gave me the explanation of Monsieur Vernisson's movements: 'Here lies Angélique who died on March the fourth.' Alexandre loved her and mourns for her!"

The worthy abbé's eyes filled with tears.

"You can see now why Monsieur Vernisson is so afraid lest Madame Honorine should learn of his present plight. What would her attitude be on hearing that her faithless husband is suspected of theft on account of his late beloved?"

Poor Monsieur Vernisson was mourning openly—partly no doubt for Angélique, and even more at the thought of his wife's wrath. His concern was all with this aspect of the affair, and he seemed oblivious of the main issue. Béchoux, the baron and the Abbé Dessole all listened intently.

"This," Barnett went on, "solves one of the problems confronting us—I mean Monsieur Vernisson's exactly timed visits to Vaneuil. This solution leads us logically up to that of the second riddle—who stole the treasure? The two are interdependent. You will readily admit that the existence of such a valuable collection is likely to rouse the imagination and excite the cupidity of many people. The idea of stealing it must have occurred occasionally to both visitors and villagers. Though, thanks to your precautions, father, the theft was made pretty difficult, yet the obstacles are quite easily surmounted by anyone who happens to know the exact nature of those precautions, and who has for years enjoyed the advantage of being able to spy out the land, plan the burglary and avoid all danger of discovery. For the crux of this kind of case is—that the thief should go unsuspected. And to avoid suspicion, there is no better stratagem than to fix suspicion on someone else … on this man, for instance, who pays furtive annual visits to the graveyard on a fixed date, who covers up his movements and invites suspicion by his very secrecy. Thus, slowly, laboriously, the plot takes shape. A grey hat, a brown overcoat, shoeprints, gold teeth—all these characteristics are the subject of minute observation by *someone*. This comparatively unknown commercial traveller is to be the culprit, while the real thief goes free. By the real thief I mean that mysterious *someone* who, secretly, perhaps in the friendly guise of a frequent visitor at the rectory, plots his ingenious manœuvre year after year."

Barnett was silent for a moment. Bit by bit he was bringing the truth to light. Monsieur Vernisson began to assume an expression of martyrdom. Barnett's hand went out to him.

"Madame Vernisson shall not know a thing about your pilgrimage, Monsieur Vernisson. Forgive the misunderstanding through which you have been made to suffer so grievously. And forgive *me* for having ransacked your gig last night and unearthed the rather amateurish hiding-place under the seat where you keep Mademoiselle Angélique's letters along with your private papers. You are a free man, Monsieur Vernisson." He loosed the other's bonds.

The commercial traveller stood up.

55

"One moment, *please!*" protested Béchoux, roused to indignation by Barnett's *dénouement*.

"Say on, Béchoux."

"What about the gold teeth?" cried the inspector, "There's no getting away from *them*. Père Dessole undoubtedly saw two gold teeth in the burglar's mouth. And Monsieur Vernisson has two gold teeth—here, on the right side. What do you make of that?"

"Those *I* saw were on the left," the abbé corrected him.

"On the right, father."

"On the left, I swear."

Jim Barnett laughed yet again.

"Shut up, both of you. You're squabbling over a trifle. Good lord, Béchoux, here are you, a police inspector, stumped by a potty little problem. Why, it's positively elementary, my poor friend. It's the sort of thing they ask the Lower Third.... Father, this room is an exact replica of your bedchamber, isn't it?"

"It is. My bedroom is directly overhead."

"Well, father, would you be so kind as to close the shutters and draw the curtains. Monsieur Vernisson, lend me your hat and coat."

Jim Barnett clapped the gray slouch hat on his head and donned the brown overcoat, turning up the collar. Then, when the room was quite dark, he produced a flashlight from his pocket and stood in front of the *curé*, projecting the beam of the torch into his own open mouth.

"The man! The man with the gold teeth!" faltered the Abbé Dessole, staring hard.

"On which side are my gold teeth, father?"

"On the right side. But—those *I* saw were on the left!"

Jim Barnett's flashlight clicked out. He seized the abbé by the shoulders and spun him round quickly several times. Then he switched on the torch again suddenly and said in a tone of command:

"Look ahead of you,... straight ahead. You can see the gold teeth, can't you? On which side are they?"

"On the left," said the abbé, utterly dumbfounded.

Jim Barnett drew back the curtains and opened the shutters.

"On the right ... on the left ... you're not quite sure, after all! Well, father, that explains what happened the other night. When you jumped out of bed, with a sleep-dazed brain, you never realized that you were facing *away* from the window and standing directly before the fireplace, so that the intruder, instead of being *in front of you*, was actually *behind you*. Therefore, when you switched on your flashlight, its beam fell not on *him* but on *his reflection in the mirror*! I've just brought about a repetition of the phenomenon by spinning you round and making you giddy. Do you see now? Or shall I dot the *i*'s of elucidation by reminding you that a mirror when it reflects an object shows you the right and left sides *reversed*? That is how you happened to see the gold teeth on the left side when they were really on the right."

"Yes!" cried Inspector Béchoux, in triumph. "But that only proves that I *was* right, and yet Père Dessole was not wrong in maintaining his assertion. Therefore it's up to you to produce a new man with gold teeth to take the place of Monsieur Vernisson."

"Quite unnecessary, I assure you."

"But you must admit that the burglar is a man with gold teeth?"

"Have *I* got gold teeth?" demanded Barnett, and took from his mouth a small piece of gold paper, which still bore the imprint of two of his teeth.

"Here's your proof. I hope you find it properly convincing. With shoeprints, a grey hat, a brown overcoat and two gold teeth, *someone* has fabricated an indisputable Monsieur Vernisson for your benefit. And how simple it is! One only has to get hold of a little bit of gilt paper—like this, which I got from the same shop in Vaneuil, where a whole sheet of it was purchased about three months ago, by the—Baron de Gravières."

Barnett's words, which he let fall quite casually, seemed to reëcho in the amazed silence which followed them. As a matter of fact, Béchoux, who had followed Barnett's line of argument pretty closely, was not altogether surprised at the climax. But the Abbé Dessole looked as though he would choke at any moment. His eyes were fixed on his estimable parishioner, the Baron de Gravières, who sat with heightened color, but said not a word. Barnett gave Monsieur Vernisson back his hat and coat. The latter mumbled as he took his leave:

"You promise faithfully, don't you, that Madame Vernisson shall never hear of this? It would be terrible if she got to know … you can imagine.…"

Barnett escorted him to the door and returned beaming. He rubbed his hands together gleefully.

"A good run and a quick kill. I feel thoroughly braced. You see how it's done, Béchoux? Just the same method I applied to the other cases where we've worked together. Never begin by accusing the man you suspect. Don't ask him to furnish an alibi. Don't even take any notice of him. *But*, while he thinks himself perfectly safe, reconstruct the case step by step in his presence. This drives him to a mental reënaction of the part he played in it. He sees what he had thought buried in dark oblivion dragged to light. He feels himself cornered, hopelessly involved, quite unable to fight against the proofs of his guilt. The ordeal is such a strain on his nerves that it scarcely occurs to him to utter a word in self-defense or protest. Isn't that so, baron? I take it we are all agreed. There's no point in going over it all again, is there? You are satisfied that my deductions are correct?"

Baron de Gravières was evidently undergoing the exact ordeal described by Barnett, for he made no attempt to confront his adversary or to conceal his own distress. His attitude was that of a criminal caught red-handed.

Jim Barnett came over and tendered affable reassurance.

"You need have no fears, monsieur. Abbé Dessole, who is anxious at all costs to avoid a scandal, only asks you to return the treasure. Once that's back in its place, the incident can be regarded as closed."

The baron raised his head, stared a moment at the man who had compassed his downfall, and, under Barnett's relentless gaze, murmured:

"There will be no prosecution? Nothing more will be said? I have your promise, father?"

"I shall say nothing, I promise," said the Abbé Dessole. "I shall blot everything from my memory the minute the treasure is restored. But I can hardly believe, even now, that *you* stole it, monsieur le baron—that *you*, whom I trusted as I would myself, should turn criminal—it's incredible!"

With the awed humility of a child confessing his sins and gaining relief by the recital, the baron whispered:

"It was too much for me, father. My thoughts kept coming back to that treasure lying there, so close ... so close ... I resisted the temptation ... I didn't want to be a thief.... Then, the whole thing seemed to take shape in my brain of its own accord...."

"I can hardly believe it!" the abbé repeated sorrowfully. "Surely—surely ——"

"It's true enough. I had lost money in rash speculation. I had nothing left to live on. Two months ago, father, I stored all my valuable antique furniture, with several grandfather clocks and some fine tapestries in my garage. I meant to sell them ... that would have been my salvation. But I couldn't bear to part with them ... and the fourth of March was so near. Temptation assailed me ... the idea of carrying out the plan that had come to me. I fell ... forgive me...."

"I forgive you," said the Abbé Dessole, "and I shall pray the Lord to be merciful in His punishment to you."

The baron stood up and said in a firm voice:

"Now, will you please come with me?"

They all walked along the highroad, like men out for a stroll. The Abbé Dessole mopped his brow. The baron's tread was heavy and his bearing bowed. Béchoux felt acute anxiety. He had little doubt that Barnett, after deftly unravelling the threads of the case, had cheerfully helped himself to the treasure.

In high feather, Barnett held forth at his side:

"How on earth you came to miss the real thief, Béchoux, beats me. You must be blind. I saw at once that Monsieur Vernisson couldn't have plotted the crime at the rate of one trip a year; that it was much more likely to be the work of a resident, and preferably of a neighbor. When I saw the neighbor!... Why, the baron's house commands an unimpeded view of church and rectory. He was familiar with the *curé's* various precautions. He knew all about Monsieur Vernisson's annual pilgrimage on the fourth of March. Then...."

But Béchoux was not listening. He was too much taken up with his fears, which solemn meditation did nothing to mitigate.

Barnett went jestingly on:

"Then, when I was sure of my case, I denounced the criminal to his face. I had no actual proof at all—nothing that would stand in a court of law. But I observed my man's face as I built up the story of what had happened and saw that he was almost beside himself. Ah, Béchoux, that's a grand and glorious feeling! And you see where it has landed us?"

"Yes, I see ... or rather, I soon shall see ... you in clover and me in the soup, I expect," said Béchoux, morbidly resigned to the ultimate doom.

Baron de Gravières had led them the length of several ditches on his estate, and they were now taking a narrow grass path across a field. He stopped short a few minutes later, near a clump of oaks.

"There," he said in a staccato voice, "in that field on the right ... in the haystack."

Béchoux's mouth wore a twisted smile. Feeling he might as well get it over, he darted to the haystack, followed by the others.

The haystack was quite a small one. In a minute, Béchoux had tumbled the top layer to the ground. Then he rummaged in the hay, working like a ferret. Suddenly he gave a shout of triumph.

"Here they are! A monstrance!" his arm brandished it clear of the hay. "A candlestick! A sconce!" he burrowed fiercely. "Six things ... no, seven."

"There should be nine!" cried the abbé.

"Nine there are! Why, they're all here! Bully for you, Barnett. Bless you, old son."

Overcome with joy, and gathering the beloved objects to his ample bosom, the abbé murmured:

"Mr. Barnett, you have my profound thanks. Heaven will reward you."

Barnett's inscrutable smile at this remark was perhaps indicative of his belief in the old saying: "Heaven helps those who help themselves."

Inspector Béchoux had been right in expecting an unpleasant surprise, only it came a little later.

On their return, as the baron and his companions again skirted the farm, they heard cries coming from the orchard. The baron rushed to the garage, in front of which three of his employees stood gesticulating.

He guessed at once what had happened. The door of the small stable adjoining the garage had been forced open and all the valuable antique furniture, the grandfather clocks and the tapestries stored there—the baron's last resources—had disappeared. He reeled back, stammering:

"This is ghastly! When did it happen?"

"Last night," said a servant. "We heard the dogs barking about eleven o'clock."

"But how could all the things have been spirited away?"

"In your car, sir."

"In my car! They've stolen that too...."

The wretched baron sank into the arms of the priest, who comforted him as best he could.

"God's punishment has not tarried, my poor friend. Accept it with a contrite heart...."

Béchoux advanced on Barnett with clenched fists, ready to spring and strike.

"You must notify the police, monsieur le baron," he rasped, in a tone of fury. "I can assure you that your furniture is not lost."

"Of course not," agreed Barnett amicably. "But to prefer a charge would be most dangerous for the baron."

Béchoux continued his measured advance. His eyes were steely, and his attitude one of threat. But Barnett drew him gently aside.

"Don't you realize what would have happened without me? The *curé* would not have got his treasure back. The innocent Vernisson would be in jail and Madame Vernisson would know all about her unfortunate husband's backsliding. The only thing left for you in the circumstances would have been to jump into the Seine."

Béchoux sank limply down upon a tree stump. He was inarticulate with rage.

"Quick, quick!" cried Barnett. "Something to pull Béchoux round.... He's not feeling well!"

Baron de Gravières gave an order. A bottle of old wine was opened. Béchoux drank down one glass, the *curé* another. The baron finished the bottle....

60

CHAPTER VI

TWELVE LITTLE NEGRO BOYS

Monsieur Gassire's first waking thought that morning was for the safety of the bundle of securities which he had brought home the previous evening. He stretched out an exploring hand, and encountered the bundle still safely on the little table by his bed.

His mind set at rest, he proceeded to get out of bed and begin the business of dressing for the day.

Nicolas Gassire was a short, corpulent man with a shriveled hawk-face. He was an outside broker doing business in the Invalides quarter of Paris, with a sound clientele of worthy bourgeois. These latter entrusted their savings to him and were rewarded by the singularly attractive profits he netted for them, in part from lucky speculations and in part from his own little private business of money-lending.

He had a flat on the first floor of a narrow old house of which he was the owner. This flat comprised a hall, his bedroom, a dining-room which he used as his office, and another room in which his three clerks worked. Right at the back there was the kitchen.

Gassire's economy led him to do without a servant. Every morning at eight the concierge, a stout, cheerful, active woman, came up with his post and *petit déjeuner*—a cup of coffee and a *croissant*, which she laid on his desk—and then cleaned up the flat.

On the morning in question the concierge departed at half-past eight, and Monsieur Gassire, as was his custom, breakfasted in leisurely fashion, opened his letters and glanced through the morning paper while he awaited the arrival of his clerks.

Suddenly, just five minutes before nine, he thought he heard a noise in his bedroom. Remembering the bundle of securities which he had left in there, he jumped up, overturning his coffee-cup in his agitation. In a twinkling he was in the other room, but—the bundle of securities had vanished! At the very same moment he heard the hall-door on the landing slam violently.

Monsieur Gassire tried to open it, but it was a spring lock and he had left the key on his desk. He was afraid that if he went to get it the thief would escape without being seen.

He therefore opened the hall window, which gave on the street. It was physically impossible for any one to have had time to leave the building. In any case, the street was empty.

Mastering his excitement, Monsieur Nicolas Gassire refrained from crying "Thief!" But, a minute later, when he caught sight of his head clerk coming towards the house from the direction of the neighboring boulevard, he beckoned furiously to him.

"Hurry up, Sarlonat!" he cried, leaning out of the window. "Come in, lock the street door and don't let any one out. I've been robbed!"

As soon as his commands had been obeyed, he hastened downstairs, panting and distraught.

"Tell me, Sarlonat, have you seen anybody?"

"Not a soul, monsieur."

He hurried to the concierge's little room, which was wedged between the foot of the stairs and a small, dark courtyard. She was sweeping the floor.

"Madame Alain, I've been robbed!" he cried. "Is any one hiding here?"

"Why, no, monsieur," faltered the poor woman in utter bewilderment.

"Where do you keep the key to my flat?"

"I put it here, monsieur, behind the clock. Anyhow, no one could have taken it, for I've not stirred out of my room this last half-hour."

"That means that instead of coming down the thief must have run upstairs. Oh, this is terrible, terrible!"

Nicolas Gassire went back to the street door. His other two clerks had just come on the scene. Hurriedly, in a few breathless words, he gave them their orders. They were to let no one enter or leave the house until he came back.

"You understand, Sarlonat? *No one.*"

He dashed upstairs and into his flat. In an instant he had grabbed hold of the telephone.

"Hello!" he bawled into the mouthpiece, "hello! Put me through to the *Préfecture*!... No, I don't mean police headquarters, you fool, I mean the *café de la Préfecture* ... what number is it?... How should I know?... Hurry!... Give me information.... Oh, be quick, be quick, can't you!"

Dancing with rage the little man at last succeeded in getting on to the proprietor of the café, and thundered:

"Is Inspector Béchoux there? Then call him to the telephone—at once. Hurry ... hurry! I want him on business. There's no time to lose.... Hello!... Inspector Béchoux? This is Gassire speaking, Béchoux.... Yes, I'm all right ... at least, I'm not ... I've just been robbed of some securities

—a whole bundle.... I'm waiting for you.... What's that? Say it again!... You can't come? You're off on your holiday? Holiday be hanged, man! Béchoux, you must come, as quickly as possible! Your twelve African mining shares were in the bundle!"

Monsieur Gassire heard a volcanic monosyllable at the other end, which fully reassured him on the score of Inspector Béchoux's purpose and promptitude. Indeed, it was barely a quarter of an hour before Inspector Béchoux arrived, running, his face a study in abject anxiety. He rushed up to the stockbroker.

"My Nigger Boys! My Twelve Little Nigger Boys! All my savings! What's become of them?"

"Stolen, along with the bonds and shares of other clients ... and all my own securities."

"Stolen?"

"Yes, from my bedroom, half an hour ago!"

"Damnation! But what were my Nigger Boys doing in your room?"

"I took the bundle out of the safe at the Crédit Lyonnais yesterday to deposit it at another bank, nearer here. And I made the mistake of——"

Béchoux's hand descended heavily on the other's shoulder.

"I shall hold you responsible, Gassire. You will have to make good my loss."

"How can I? I'm ruined."

"What do you mean? You have this house."

"Mortgaged to the hilt!"

The two men faced each other, convulsed with rage and shouting unintelligibly.

The concierge and the three clerks had also lost their heads, and were barring the way to two girls from the top floor, who had just come down and were quite determined to be allowed out.

"Nobody shall leave this house!" roared Béchoux, beside himself with fury. "Nobody shall leave this house until my Twelve Little Nigger Boys are restored to me!"

"Perhaps we'd better call in help," suggested Gassire. "There's the butcher's boy ... and the grocer ... they're both dependable."

"Not for me," the inspector pronounced with decision. "If we need some one else we'll telephone the Barnett Agency in the *rue Laborde*. Then we'll notify the police. But for the moment that would be sheer waste of time. Action is what we want!"

He tried to control himself and to regain the pontifical calm that best befits a police inspector. But he was trembling from head to foot, and his quivering mouth betrayed his distress.

"Keep your head," he told Gassire. "After all, we have the whip hand. Nobody has left the house. The thing is to retrieve my little Nigger Boys before any one can find a way of sneaking them out of the building. That's all that really matters."

He turned to the two girls and began to question them. He ascertained that one was a typist who copied reports and circulars at home. The other gave lessons in flute-playing, also at home. They were both anxious to get out and do their marketing before lunch, but Béchoux was adamant.

"I'm sorry," he said, "but this door stays closed for the morning. Monsieur Gassire, two of your clerks shall mount guard here. The third can run errands for the tenants. In the afternoon the latter will be allowed out, but with my permission only in each case, and all parcels, boxes, baskets or packages of any kind will be submitted to a rigorous search. You have your orders. Now, Monsieur Gassire, it is for us to get to work. The concierge will lead the way."

The building was so planned as to make investigation easy. There were three upper stories, with a single flat on each floor. This made four flats in the house, counting that on the ground floor, which was temporarily unoccupied. Monsieur Gassire lived on the first floor. On the second dwelt Monsieur Touffémont, an ex-Cabinet Minister. The top floor was partitioned off into two flatlets, occupied by Mademoiselle Legoffier, the typist, and Mademoiselle Haveline, who taught the flute.

That morning Monsieur Touffémont had left at half-past eight for the *Chambre des Députés*, where he was president of a commission. Since his flat was cleaned by a woman who came in daily at lunch-time and had not yet arrived, they decided to await his return.

First, then, they explored the girls' rooms thoroughly, and satisfied themselves that the missing securities were not there.

Next they searched every corner of the attic at the top of the house, getting up there by means of a ladder.

After this, choking with dust, they came downstairs again and searched the courtyard and Monsieur Gassire's own flat.

Their efforts went unrewarded. In bitterness of spirit, Béchoux brooded over the unkind fate that had overtaken his Twelve Little Nigger Boys.

Towards noon Monsieur Touffémont came in. He proved to be an earnest parliamentarian, burdened with the type of portfolio proper to the use of an ex-Cabinet Minister. His industry commanded the respect of all parties in the house, and his rare but masterly interventions could make a Cabinet tremble apprehensively.

With measured tread he approached the concierge's room and asked for his letters. Gassire came up to him and told him of the theft.

Touffémont gave him that grave attention he seemed to bestow even on the most flippant utterances. Then he promised his coöperation if Gassire decided to call in the police, and urged at the same time that they should search his flat.

"You never know," he said. "Someone might have got in with a skeleton key."

Accordingly they searched the flat, but here again they drew a blank. Béchoux and Gassire tried to keep one another's courage up by voicing each in turn his meed of hope and comfort, but their words rang hollow and their faces grew drawn and pale.

At last they thought they would go in search of refreshment to a small café just opposite, so placed that they could keep an eye on the home all the time. But when they got there, Béchoux found he had no appetite. The Twelve Little Nigger Boys lay heavy on his stomach. Gassire said that *he* felt dizzy. No, he wouldn't take anything, thank you. They both went over and over what had happened, trying to find some ray of reassurance in the prevailing gloom.

"It's quite obvious," said Béchoux. "Someone got into your flat and stole the securities. Well, as the thief can't have escaped from the building, that means that he or she is still in the house."

"Absolutely," agreed Gassire.

"And if he or she is in the house, my Twelve Little Nigger Boys are there too. Hang it all, they can't have flown out through the roof!"

"Not unless they were nigger angels," suggested Gassire.

"So," Béchoux went on, ignoring him, "we are forced to the conclusion that——"

He never finished the sentence. Suddenly a look of terror came into his eyes, and he stared speechless at someone who was jauntily approaching the house opposite.

"Barnett!" he whispered. "Barnett! How did *he* get to know of this?"

"You mentioned him, and the Barnett Agency in the *rue Laborde*," Gassire confessed, not without hesitation, "and I thought that, in the appalling circumstances, it was just worth giving him a ring."

"You fool!" spluttered Béchoux. "Who's in charge of the case, anyhow? You or me? Barnett has nothing to do with this. We must be on our guard against him or there will be the devil to pay. Let Barnett in on this? Not much!"

Béchoux was quite sure in his own mind that Barnett's assistance would prove the last straw. Jim Barnett in the house and on the case would only mean that, if the mystery were solved, a bundle of securities, including Twelve Little Nigger Boys of vital import to their owner, would surely vanish into thin air.

He tore across the street, and, as Barnett raised his hand to the bell, he seized his arm and said in trembling tones:

"Get out! Hop it! We don't want your help. You were called in by mistake. Cut along now, and be quick about it."

Barnett gave him an astonished stare full of reproach and childlike innocence.

"My dear Béchoux, what's the matter? Tell your Uncle Barnett! You seem a trifle rattled, old lad. Still sore about the grandfather clocks of Baron de Gravières? And those gold teeth? Left, right!"

"Get out, I tell you!"

"Then they told me the truth just now on the telephone? Have you really been robbed of your savings? And don't you want your Uncle Barnett to lend a helping hand?"

"My Uncle Barnett can go to hell!" declared Béchoux, furious. "I know all about your helping hand! It goes into other people's pockets and helps itself."

"Are you in a stew because of your Twelve Little Nigger Boys?"

"I shall be if *you* come poking your nose in!"

"Oh, all right. I leave you to it!"

"You're off, then?" Béchoux's frown cleared.

"Rather not! I've come here on business."

He turned to Gassire, who had joined them and was holding the door ajar.

"Can you tell me if Mademoiselle Haveline lives here—Mademoiselle Haveline who teaches the flute? She took second prize at the Conservatoire."

Béchoux grew wrathful.

"Huh, you're asking for her because you've just seen her brass plate up there...."

"Well," replied Barnett, "haven't I a perfect right to learn the flute if I like? It's a free country!"

"You can't come here."

"Sorry, but I am consumed with a passion for the flute."

"I absolutely forbid it."

For sole answer Barnett snapped his fingers in the other's face and pushed past him into the house. No one dared bar his way. Béchoux, his heart full of misgivings, watched him ascend the first flight of stairs and vanish out of sight.

It must have taken Barnett only a little while to get started with his teacher, for in ten minutes' time wobbly scales on the flute began floating down from the top floor. Mademoiselle Haveline's pupil was on the job!

66

"The scoundrel!" cried Béchoux, his anxiety increasing every minute. "With him in the house, heaven help us!"

He set to work again madly. They ransacked the empty ground floor flat, also the concierge's room, in case the bundle of securities had been thrown down somewhere. It was all fruitless. And the whole afternoon the sound of flute practice went on, like a mocking goblin under the eaves. Béchoux nearly collapsed beneath the strain.

At last, on the stroke of six, Barnett appeared, skipping down the stairs and humming a ribald tune. And, as he went, he swung to and fro a large cardboard box.

A cardboard box! Béchoux, with a strangled exclamation, seized it and snatched off the lid. Out tumbled some old hat-shapes and bits of moth-eaten fur.

"Since she is not allowed to leave the house," Barnett explained solemnly, "Mademoiselle Haveline has asked me to throw this stuff away for her. I say, isn't she a peach? And what a flautist! She thinks I am full of talent and says that if I keep on at it I shall soon be able to qualify for the post of blind man on the church steps. Ta, ta!" And he was gone.

All night long, Béchoux and Gassire mounted guard, one inside and the other outside the street door, in case the thief should try to throw a parcel out of a window to an accomplice waiting below. And next day they set to work again, but all in vain.

At three o'clock that afternoon Barnett was on the scene again, carrying the empty cardboard box. He went straight upstairs, nodding affably to poor Béchoux in the manner of one whose time is well and fully occupied.

The flute lesson began. Scales, followed by exercises. The critical listener would have detected plenty of wrong notes.

Suddenly all was quiet. The silence continued unbroken, until Béchoux was thoroughly puzzled.

"What on earth can he be up to now?" he wondered, as he pictured Barnett busy with those private researches which would assuredly culminate in some extraordinary discovery.

He ran upstairs and stood listening on the landing. No sound came from Mademoiselle Haveline's room. But a man's voice was distinctly audible in the next door flatlet of Mademoiselle Legoffier, the typist.

"Barnett's voice," thought Béchoux, his curiosity now at white-heat. Then, incapable of holding back any longer, he rang the bell.

"Come in!" called Barnett from within. "The key is in the lock outside."

Béchoux entered the room. Mademoiselle Legoffier, an attractive brunette, was sitting at a table by her typewriter, taking shorthand at Barnett's dictation.

"The hunt is up, is it?" said the latter. "Carry on, old man. Nothing up my sleeves"—he mimicked a conjurer—"and as for Mademoiselle Legoffier——" That damsel blushed discreetly; her arms were bare to the shoulder.

"Well," Barnett continued, "I'm dictating my memoirs. You won't mind if I go on?"

And, while Béchoux peered under the furniture, he proceeded:

"That afternoon Inspector Béchoux dropped in while I was dictating my memoirs to a charming young lady called Legoffier. She had been recommended to me by her friend, the flautist. Béchoux searched high and low for his Twelve Little Nigger Boys, who heartlessly persisted in eluding him. Under the couch he collected three grains of dust; under the wardrobe a shoe-heel and a hairpin. Inspector Béchoux never overlooks the slightest detail. What a life!"

Béchoux stood up and shook his fist in Barnett's face, volleying abuse. The other went on dictating, and the detective departed in a fury.

A little later Barnett came down with his cardboard box. Béchoux, who was keeping watch, had a moment's hesitation. But his fears conquered him and he opened the box, to find that it contained nothing but old papers and rags.

Life became unbearable for the unhappy Béchoux. Barnett's continued presence, his quizzical attitude and freakish pranks threw the detective into fresh fits of rage. Every day Barnett came to the house, and after each flute lesson or shorthand séance, he would display his cardboard box.

Béchoux did not know what to do. He had no doubt that the whole thing was a farce and that Barnett was ragging him. All the same, there was always the chance that this time Barnett really *was* spiriting away the securities. Suppose he was kidnapping the Twelve Little Nigger Boys? Suppose he was smuggling his haul out of the house?

Béchoux was forced to rummage in the box, empty it and run his hands over its oddly assorted contents of torn clothing, rags, old feather dusters, broom handles, ashes and potato peelings. And this made Barnett roar with laughter.

"He's found his shares! No, false alarm! He's getting warm … try that lettuce leaf! Ah, Béchoux, what a lot of quiet fun you manage to give me, bless you!"

This went on for a week. Béchoux lost the whole of his holiday over the wretched business, and made himself the laughing-stock of the neighborhood. For neither he nor Nicolas Gassire had been able to stop the tenants from attending to their own affairs, even while allowing their persons to be searched on exit and entrance. Gossip travelled apace. Gassire's misfortune became known. His terrified clients flocked to the office and demanded the immediate return of their money.

As for Monsieur Touffémont, the ex-Cabinet Minister, who came under the amateur surveillance four times a day, to his great annoyance and the interruption of his customary routine, *he* was all for calling in the police officially, and urged Gassire to take this course without further delay. The situation could not be prolonged indefinitely.

At last things came to a head. Late one afternoon Gassire and Béchoux heard sounds of violent quarreling coming from the top of the house. Two high-pitched voices were raised in rival but continuous clamor, the uproar punctuated by stamps and screams. It sounded most alarming.

The two men hurried upstairs. On the top landing Mademoiselle Haveline and Mademoiselle Legoffier were doing battle. Standing over them like an umpire was Jim Barnett!

Although quite unable to restrain the combatants, Barnett wore an expression of genuine enjoyment. The girls continued to fly at each other, their hair like that of Furies, and their frocks getting torn to shreds. The air was thick with Parisienne invective!

After heroic efforts the pair was separated. The typist promptly went into hysterics, and Barnett carried her into her flat, while the flute teacher proceeded to expound her wrongs to Béchoux and Gassire on the landing.

"Caught them together, I did," shrilled Mademoiselle Haveline. "Barnett was mine first, and then I caught him kissing *her*! I can tell you, he's up to no good, that Barnett. He's a queer sort and no mistake. Why don't you ask him, Monsieur Béchoux, what his game's been up here all this week, questioning the two of us and poking his nose everywhere? I'm going to give him away, though. *He* knows who the thief is. It's the concierge, Madame Alain. But he made us swear we wouldn't let on to you. Another thing, he knows where those securities are. Didn't he tell us: 'The securities are in the house, and yet not in it, and they're out of it, and yet in it'? Those were his very words. You want to be careful of him, Monsieur Béchoux!"

Jim Barnett had finished with the typist and now came forth. Taking Mademoiselle Haveline by the shoulders, he pushed her firmly through her own front door.

"Come along, professor mine, and no idle gossip, *if* you please! You're going right off the handle. Stop talking nonsense and stick to the flute. I don't want you playing in *my* band!"

Béchoux did not stay any longer. Mademoiselle Haveline's sudden revelation had shed a ray of light on the case. He now saw that the thief must be Madame Alain. He only marveled that he could ever have overlooked her guilt.

Spurred by his conviction, he rushed downstairs, followed by Nicolas Gassire, and burst in upon the concierge.

"My Africans! Where are they? It was you who stole them!"

Nicolas Gassire panted at his heels.

"My securities! Where have you put them, you thief?"

They each took hold of the poor woman, shaking her violently and over-whelming her with abuse and questions. She seemed quite dazed by it all, but stuck bravely to her protestations of innocence and ignorance.

When at last they let her be, she retired to bed and passed a sleepless night. Next morning the inquisition recommenced, and that day and its successor were long hours of unrelieved ordeal for the poor woman.

Béchoux would not for a minute admit that Jim Barnett could have made a mistake. Besides, in the light of this definite accusation, it was easy to put the right construction on the facts of the case. The concierge, while cleaning the flat, had doubtless noticed the unaccustomed bundle on the table by the bed. She was the only person who had the key to the flat. Knowing Monsieur Gassire's regular habits, she might well have returned to the flat, seized the securities, run off with them, and taken refuge in the little room where Nicolas Gassire found her when he rushed downstairs.

Béchoux began to get discouraged.

"Yes," he said, "it's obvious that this woman is the guilty party. But still we're no nearer a solution of the mystery. I don't care if the criminal is the concierge or the man in the moon. It makes no odds as long as we are still without news of my Twelve Little Nigger Boys. I can see that she had them in her room, but by what miracle did they leave it between nine o'clock and the time we searched her belongings?"

All their threats, and the "third degree" cross-examination to which she was subjected failed to make the fat Madame Alain disclose any helpful information. She denied everything. She had seen nothing. She knew nothing. Even though there was now no doubt of her guilt she stood firm.

"We've simply got to settle this," Gassire told Béchoux one morning. "You know that Touffémont overthrew the Cabinet last night. The reporters will be here any minute to interview him, and we can't possibly go searching them, too."

Béchoux agreed that they had come to an impasse.

"But keep smiling," he urged, "for within three hours I shall know the truth."

That afternoon he called at the Barnett Detective Agency.

"I was waiting for you to drop in, Béchoux," said Barnett amicably. "What do you want?"

"I want your coöperation, Barnett. I'm at a loss what to do."

70

This was unvarnished admission of defeat. The inspector's surrender was unconditional. Béchoux was making the *amende honorable*.

Jim Barnett clapped him friendliwise on the back, then took him by the shoulders and rocked him gently to and fro, by sheer geniality sparing the other humiliation. This was no meeting of vanquished and victor. Rather was it a scene of reconciliation between two comrades.

"To tell you the truth, Béchoux, I was awfully cut up about that misunderstanding between us. I couldn't bear to think of our being enemies. It worried me till I could hardly sleep at nights!"

A frown clouded Béchoux's brow. His professional conscience pricked him sore for being on friendly terms with Barnett. He cursed the unkind fate that forced him to collaborate with a man he felt sure was a crook, and to incur obligations to the fellow into the bargain. But there are moments and circumstances when even the just man stretches a point. The loss of a dozen valuable African mining shares explained Béchoux's course of action.

Swallowing his scruples, he whispered:

"It's the concierge, of course?"

"It is she for the reason, *inter alia*, that it could not be any one else."

"But how do you account for a woman who has always been honest and respectable suddenly turning crook?"

"If you had troubled to make a few inquiries about her you would know that the poor creature is afflicted with a son who is a thorough bad hat. He is always sponging on her. It was on his account that she suddenly gave way to temptation."

Béchoux jumped up.

"Did she manage to give him my shares?" he asked anxiously.

"Of course not! Do you think I should have allowed a thing like that? I regard your Twelve Little Nigger Boys as sacred."

"Where are they, then?"

"In your own coat-pocket."

"Please don't joke about it."

"But, Béchoux, I'm *not* joking. I never joke in times of stress. Look for yourself!"

Béchoux's hand went gingerly to his coat-pocket, felt in it and took out a large envelope which bore the following superscription: "To my friend Béchoux." With trembling fingers he tore it open. Oh, joy, his Nigger Boys were restored to him, all twelve! Clutching the precious shares to his breast, he turned very pale and closed his eyes. Barnett hastened to revive him with smelling salts held under the nose.

"Sniff hard, Béchoux. This is no time to faint."

Béchoux did not faint, though he surreptitiously wiped away a few tears of relief. He was inarticulate with emotion. Of course he had no doubt but that Barnett had stuffed the envelope into his pocket the moment he came into the Agency, while they were making up their differences. But anyhow there were the Twelve Little Nigger Boys in his still trembling hands, and Barnett's virtue was for him untarnished.

Reviving suddenly, he began capering about, dancing a kind of Spanish jig shaking imaginary castanets.

"I've got them back! My own little pickaninnies! Bless you, Barnett, for a friend in need. From now on there is only one Barnett—Béchoux's pre-server! You deserve a statue *and* a drinking fountain. You are one of our truly great men. But how on earth did you bring it off? Tell me all."

Once again Barnett's little way was a source of amazement to Inspector Béchoux. His professional curiosity thoroughly aroused, he asked:

"Won't you tell me?"

"Tell you what?" Barnett's tone was one of amused indolence.

"How you unravelled everything! Where was the bundle? 'In the house yet out of it,' was what you said, I believe?"

"'And out of the house but in it,'" added Barnett with a laugh.

"What *does* it mean?"

"D'you give it up?"

"Yes, yes; I give it up. I'll do anything you ask."

"Will you promise never again to take up that chilly and reproachful attitude towards my harmless exploits, which almost convinces me at times that I must have wandered from the straight and narrow path?"

"Go on, tell me, Barnett!"

"Ah," exclaimed the other, "*what* a story! I've never come across anything more neatly done, more unexpected, more spontaneous or more baffling. It was at once human and fantastic. And withal so simple that you, Béchoux, gifted as you are in your profession, were absolutely in the dark."

"Well, hang it all, come to the point," said Béchoux in some annoyance. "How did the bundle of securities leave the house?"

"Under your own eyes, my bright lad! And not only did it leave the house, but it came in again. It left the house twice daily, and twice daily it returned! And under your own eyes, Béchoux, under your bright, benignant eyes! And for ten days you bowed to it respectfully. You almost grovelled on your knees before it!"

"I don't believe you!" cried Béchoux. "It's absurd. We searched everything."

"Everything was searched, Béchoux, except that. Parcels, boxes, handbags, pockets, hats, tins, dustbins ... all those, but not *that*. At the frontier they search all luggage, except the diplomat's valise. Naturally, you searched everything but that."

"What is *that*?" yelled Béchoux frenziedly. "For goodness sake, answer me."

"The portfolio of the ex-Cabinet Minister!"

Béchoux sprang up in astonishment.

"What do you mean, Barnett? Are you accusing Monsieur Touffémont?"

"Idiot, should I dare accuse a member of parliament? In the first place, that man, an ex-Cabinet Minister, is above suspicion. And among all members of parliament and ex-Cabinet Ministers—and Lord knows their name is legion—I regard Touffémont as the least open to suspicion. All the same, Madame Alain made him a receiver of stolen goods!"

"Then he was her accomplice?"

"Not a bit of it!"

"Then who was?"

"His portfolio!" And, with a broad smile, Barnett proceeded to elucidate. "A minister's portfolio, Béchoux, has a personality of its own. In this world we have Monsieur Touffémont and we have his portfolio. The two are inseparable, and each is the other's *raison d'être*. You can't imagine Monsieur Touffémont minus his portfolio—nor the portfolio minus Monsieur Touffémont. But it happens that Monsieur Touffémont lays down his portfolio when he eats and sleeps, and on various other occasions through the day. At such times the portfolio assumes a separate identity and may lend itself to actions for which Monsieur Touffémont cannot be held responsible.

"That was what happened on the morning of the theft."

Béchoux stared at Barnett, wondering what on earth he was getting at.

"That was what happened," Barnett repeated, "on the morning that your twelve African mining shares vanished away. The concierge, terrified by what she had done, and dreading the consequences of her action, could not think how to get rid of the securities, which were bound to betray her guilt. Suddenly she noticed the providential presence of Monsieur Touffémont's portfolio on her mantelpiece—the portfolio all by itself! Monsieur Touffémont had come in there to collect his post. He put his portfolio down on the mantelpiece and proceeded to open his letters, while Gassire and you, Béchoux, were telling him about the disappearance of the securities.

"Then Madame Alain had an inspiration of sheer genius. Her room had not yet been searched, but it was bound to be ransacked in a little while, and the securities would be discovered. She had no time to lose. She turned her back on the three of you standing there discussing the theft. With quick, deft fingers she opened the portfolio, emptied one of the flap pockets of all its papers, and slipped the securities into their place. The deed was done, the great bell rung. No one suspected anything. And when Monsieur Touffémont withdrew, he took away in the portfolio under his arm your Twelve Little Nigger Boys and all Gassire's securities."

Béchoux never questioned Barnett's asseverations when they were made on that particular note of absolute conviction. Instead, he bowed his head humbly in the Temple of Truth and believed what he was told.

"Certainly," he said, "I noticed a sheaf of papers and reports lying about down there that morning, but I paid no attention to it. And surely she must have given those documents back to Monsieur Touffémont?"

"I hardly think so," answered Barnett. "Rather than incur any suspicion she probably burned them."

"But *he* must have asked after them?"

Barnett shook his head and smiled quietly.

"You mean to say he hasn't noticed the disappearance of a whole sheaf of his papers?"

"Has he noticed the appearance of the bundle of securities?"

"But—but what happened when he opened the portfolio?"

"He didn't open it. He never opens it. Monsieur Touffémont's portfolio, like that of many a politician, is only a sham—a dummy—a useful prop on the parliamentary stage. If he had opened it he would have demanded the return of his own papers, and restored the securities. He has done neither."

"But when he works...."

"He doesn't work. The mere fact of a man's carrying a portfolio does not necessarily imply that he works. As a matter of fact, the possession of an ex-minister's portfolio is in itself a dispensation from work. A portfolio stands for power, authority, omnipotence, and omniscience. Last night, at the *Chambre des Députés*—I was there myself, by the way—Monsieur Touffémont laid down his portfolio on the rostrum. You can see that his doing this at such a crisis was tantamount to announcing publicly that he was once again a candidate for office. The Cabinet realized that it was lost. The great man's portfolio must be full of crushing documents crammed with statistics! Monsieur Touffémont even undid it, though he took nothing from its bulging compartments. It was so obvious that he had everything there.... But really, there was nothing there except your twelve African mining shares, Gassire's securities and some old newspapers. They carried the day, however, and Monsieur Touffémont's portfolio overthrew the Cabinet."

"But how do you know all this?"

"Because, when Monsieur Touffémont was strolling home from the House at one o'clock in the morning, a person unknown came into clumsy collision with him and sent him sprawling on the pavement. Another man—an accomplice—snatched up the portfolio and replaced the securities with a bundle of old papers, carrying off the former. Need I tell you the name of the second man?"

Béchoux laughed heartily. Every time his hand felt the twelve shares in his pocket he was struck afresh with the humor of the story and of Monsieur Touffémont's little adventure.

Barnett, beaming on his friend, concluded:

"That's all there is to know, and it was in my endeavor to ferret out the truth and collect evidence in the case that I've dictated my memoirs and taken lessons on the flute. What a pleasant week it's been! Flirtations up above and a variety entertainment on the ground floor. Gassire, Béchoux, Madame Alain, Touffémont … my own little marionettes, dancing when I pulled the strings! The hardest nut I had to crack was that Touffémont could actually be oblivious of his portfolio's guilty secret, and be taking your Twelve Little Nigger Boys to and fro in blissful ignorance. At first it had me absolutely beat. And how surprised the poor concierge must have been! She must think Touffémont a common crook, since she certainly believes that he has stuck to your Little Nigger Boys and the rest of the bundle. Fancy Touffémont——"

"Hadn't I better tell him?" broke in Béchoux.

"What's the good? Let him go on carting his old newspapers about and sleeping with the portfolio under his pillow. Don't let on about this to anyone, Béchoux."

"Except Gassire, of course," said Béchoux. "I shall have to explain to him when I give him back his securities."

"What securities?" asked Barnett blankly.

"The ones you found in Monsieur Touffémont's portfolio—they're his!"

"You must be crazy, Béchoux. You don't suppose Gassire will ever see his securities again?"

"Naturally I do."

Barnett brought his fist down on the table and gave vent to a sudden burst of righteous indignation.

"Look here, Béchoux, do you know what sort of man Nicolas Gassire is? He's a scoundrel like the concierge's son! He robbed his clients—I can prove it! He gambled with their money. He was even preparing to steal the lot. Look, here is his first-class railway ticket to Brussels. He bought it on the same day that he withdrew the securities from his safe deposit, not to hand them over to another bank as he told you, but to bolt with them! How do you feel about Nicolas Gassire now?"

Béchoux could say nothing. Ever since the theft of his shares his confidence in Nicolas Gassire had been considerably shaken. Still, he raised the obvious objection.

"His clients are all decent people. It's not fair to ruin them as well."

"Who ever talked of ruining them? That would be disgraceful. It would upset me terribly!"

Béchoux looked his interrogation.

"Gassire is rich," observed Barnett.

"He's broke," contradicted Béchoux.

"Not at all. I have information that he has enough money to pay back all his clients and then leave something over. You can be quite sure that the reason he didn't call in the police the very first day was that he didn't want them meddling in his private affairs. Threaten him with imprisonment, and watch him skip! Why, Nicolas Gassire is a millionaire. It's up to him to right his client's wrongs, no business of mine!"

"Which means that you intend keeping the securities?"

"Certainly not! They're already sold!"

"Yes, but you've got the cash."

Barnett was virtuously indignant and protested that he had kept nothing.

"I'm merely distributing it," he declared.

"To whom?"

"To friends in distress and to various deserving charities which I supply with funds. You needn't worry, Béchoux. I'm making good use of Gassire's money."

Béchoux did not doubt it. Yet another treasure-hunt in which the prize was forfeit at the finish! Barnett, as usual, walked off with the spoils. He punished the guilty and saved the innocent—and never forgot to line his pockets in the process. Well-ordered charity invariably begins at home.

Inspector Béchoux found himself blushing. If he made no protest, he became Barnett's accomplice. But, as he felt the precious bundle of shares in his pocket, and realized that without Barnett's intervention he would have lost them for ever, he cooled down. It was hardly an opportune moment to enter the lists!

"What's up?" asked Barnett. "Aren't you pleased?"

"Oh, rather," said the luckless Béchoux hastily. "Delighted!"

"Then smile, smile, smile!"

Béchoux managed a grimace like a watery sunset.

"*That's* better," cried Barnett. "It's been a pleasure to do you this small service, and I thank you for giving me the opportunity. And now it's time for us to part. You must be very busy, and I'm expecting a lady."

"So long," said Béchoux, and made for the door.

"To our next merry meeting," answered Barnett.

Béchoux took his leave, delighted, indeed, but at loggerheads with his conscience and firmly resolved to shun Barnett's society henceforward.

As he turned the corner of the *rue Laborde* he noticed the pretty typist from the Invalides hurrying along. Doubtless she was the lady Barnett was expecting!

And, a couple of days later, Béchoux saw Barnett at the cinema, accompanied by the equally charming Mademoiselle Haveline, who played upon the flute....

CHAPTER VII

THE BRIDGE THAT BROKE

It was a Tuesday afternoon in midsummer. Paris was deserted—a city of the dead. Jim Barnett sat in his office with his feet on his desk. He was in his shirt-sleeves. A glass of lager beer stood at his elbow. A green blind shut out the blazing sun. To the prejudiced eye, Barnett's appearance would have suggested slumber, and this impression would have been strengthened by his rather loud and rhythmical breathing.

A sharp tap on his door made him bring his feet down with a jerk and sit bolt upright.

"No! It can't be! The heat must be affecting my eyesight." Barnett affected elaborate astonishment.

Inspector Béchoux, for it was he, closed the door behind him and observed with some distaste his friend's state of déshabillé. It was a fad with Béchoux to present at all times a perfectly groomed appearance. On this sweltering day he was cool and immaculate, not a hair out of place.

"How *do* you do it?" Barnett demanded, sinking back wearily into his chair.

"Do what?"

"Look like a fashion-plate off the ice. Damned superior, I call it!"

Béchoux smiled with conscious pride.

"It's quite simple," he remarked modestly.

"But I take it the case you are working on is *not* quite so simple, or you wouldn't be coming to the enemy camp for assistance, eh Béchoux?"

Béchoux reddened. It was a very sore point with him that in his difficulties he had several times been forced to accept Jim Barnett's help. For Barnett *was* helpful—almost uncannily so. The trouble was that he always managed to help himself as well as others. But Béchoux felt profoundly grateful to Barnett for having retrieved these African shares—his precious Twelve Little Nigger Boys.

"What is it this time? I've all day to spare—and to-morrow—and the day after. The Barnett Agency doesn't get many clients at this time of year,

78

though it does guarantee 'Information Free.' I hear that they can't even get deadheads to go to the theatres—pouf!"

"How would you like a trip into the country?"

"Béchoux, you are a blessing, albeit heavily disguised. What is the case, though?"

Inspector Béchoux grimaced involuntarily.

"It's a real mystery—the sudden death of the famous scientist, Professor Saint-Prix."

"I know the name, but I haven't read about his death in the papers. Has he been murdered?"

Inspector Béchoux's countenance took on a sphinx-like expression.

"That's what I want you to help me to determine. I have my car at a garage near here. Pack a bag and come right along. I'll tell you the facts of the case as we go."

Reluctantly Barnett got up, drained the last of his beer, and made his simple preparations for the trip.

A quarter of an hour later they were spinning out of Paris in Inspector Béchoux's little two-seater.

"I was called in on the case," said Béchoux, "by Doctor Desportes of Beauvray—an old friend. He rang up on Monday morning to say there was going to be an inquest at Beauvray—Professor Saint-Prix, the scientist, had been killed by falling into the stream at the bottom of his garden."

"Nothing very mysterious in that."

"Ah, but wait. The professor was crossing the stream by a plank bridge, and that bridge gave way under him and precipitated the old man into the water. His head hit a sharp rock and he was killed instantaneously."

"Was the bridge rotten, then?"

Inspector Béchoux shook his head.

"My doctor friend informed me that though the police had not been called in, they would have to be. The bridge was perfectly sound, but—it had been *sawed through*!"

Barnett whistled.

"And so you went to Beauvray at once?"

"Yes."

"And what did you find?"

"A queer situation. The professor had a little house where he lived with his daughter, Thérèse Saint-Prix. Joined on to the house was a very fine laboratory. The garden sloped down, first a lawn and then a dense shrubbery, to a stream, sunk deep between rocky banks. A stout plank bridge was the means of crossing from the Saint-Prix garden to the adjoining property of the Villa Eméraude, the home of a married couple, the Lenormands.

"Louis Lenormand is a young stockbroker. His wife, Cécile, is a delicate, beautiful girl. Last Sunday afternoon, Madame Lenormand was going to have tea with Thérèse Saint-Prix. Louis Lenormand was spending the weekend in Paris with his invalid mother, but was expected back that night.

"Madame Lenormand went through the garden of the Villa Eméraude down to the stream. When she got there, she pulled up short and gave a cry of horror! The plank bridge was broken, and in the water lay the body of Professor Saint-Prix. She rushed back to the house for help, and then fainted."

"Well, where do I come in?"

"Almost as soon as they had got Madame Lenormand to bed, and were breaking the news of her father's death to Thérèse Saint-Prix, Louis Lenormand arrived in his car, driving like a fury. He was pale and trembling. The first words he spoke were: 'Am I in time? Tell me—tell me. My God, I've been a fool!' He was like a madman and rushed upstairs to his wife's room without waiting for an answer from the astonished servants. His wife's maid told him what had happened. At first he did not seem to understand. Then he stole to his wife's bedside and kissed her hands passionately, weeping and murmuring, 'Cécile, I am a murderer.'"

"Still I confess I don't understand. You have your murder—you have your murderer, self-confessed. What more do you want?"

"Well, the thing is this. We checked up on Louis Lenormand's movements while he was away from Beauvray. We know that the bridge was perfectly safe on the Saturday morning, for a gardener crossed by it. Now all Saturday afternoon Lenormand spent at his mother's bedside. He sat with her again after dinner until eleven o'clock, and then turned into bed himself. Old Madame Lenormand's maid and cook heard him kicking off his shoes in the room next to theirs. And the maid swears that in the small hours she heard him switch off his light, so she supposes he must have been lying awake reading. All Sunday morning he did not stir out, so it is out of the question that he could possibly have sawed through the bridge between the gardens at Beauvray."

"What made you establish such a thorough alibi for your suspect?"

"Madame Lenormand, though still weak from the shock, has recovered consciousness. Her belief in her husband's innocence is absolute. Her one aim is to clear him. She insisted on these investigations being made. He will not say a word in his own defence. It's all very mystifying."

"You say that Louis Lenormand was not expected back until Sunday evening. Do you know why he left Paris so much earlier?"

"That," said Béchoux, "is a curious point. Apparently he was alone in one of the rooms in his mother's flat, reading a book while the old lady had a nap after her lunch. The servants were both in the kitchen, and testify that suddenly, at about three o'clock, he rushed into them and said he was going home at once but would not disturb his mother to say good-bye."

"And the motive? What reason could Louis Lenormand have to murder his neighbor?"

Inspector Béchoux shrugged his shoulders.

"I have an idea, and Doctor Desportes is making some investigations on my behalf."

"Is there no one else who comes under suspicion? What about Madame Lenormand?"

Inspector Béchoux was silent. The car swung off the main road up a shady avenue. They turned into the drive of the Villa Eméraude. They were met outside the house by Doctor Desportes, who announced:

"The Beauvray police have arrested Monsieur Lenormand, but I have been busy on the telephone to headquarters, and you are now officially in charge of the case."

"But his alibi—he was in Paris all the time—he could not have sawed through the bridge!"

The doctor looked grave.

"Monsieur Lenormand had a latch-key to his mother's flat. The Paris police have inquired at the garage where he kept his car and they find that he took it out shortly after midnight and told a mechanic that he was unable to sleep because of the heat, and was going to try and get a breath of air in the Bois. He returned after two in the morning."

"Which," observed Barnett, "gave him plenty of time to drive out here, saw through the bridge and get back to Paris. And what the maid heard was Monsieur Lenormand switching off his light when he really went to bed at last. Both servants must have been asleep when he slipped out of the flat."

The doctor looked at Barnett in some curiosity, for he spoke in such an assured tone and was so obviously no subordinate of Inspector Béchoux.

Barnett smiled and bowed easily.

"Allow me to remedy my friend Béchoux's deplorable lack of manners. Jim Barnett, at your service, doctor."

"A friend of mine, who has helped me on more than one occasion," said Béchoux, not so easily. "Come, doctor, what news have you for me after your confidential interview with the bank manager at Beauvray?"

"Poor Monsieur Lenormand." The doctor shook his head sadly. "I wish it had been a policeman who had found it out. But justice cannot be cheated. I have established that for the past two years Monsieur Lenormand has from time to time paid quite large checks into the banking account of Professor Saint-Prix."

"Blackmail?" Barnett and Béchoux came out with the word simultaneously.

"There we have at last the motive!" cried Béchoux, in purely professional triumph. "Monsieur Lenormand must have had a very good reason for sawing through that bridge——"

"But he did not do it!"

A young woman, deathly pale, wearing a brilliant Chinese wrap, was coming slowly down the stairs into the hall, clutching at the banister for support. A maid followed anxiously behind her.

"I repeat," she said in a voice trembling with suppressed emotion, "Louis is innocent!"

"Madame," said Béchoux, "allow me to present my friend, Jim Barnett." Barnett bowed low. "If anyone can achieve the impossible and establish your husband's innocence, it is he! I admit, however, that I originally brought him here because your husband's alibi upset all my deductions: Now that alibi no longer holds, and I have no objection if Barnett transfers his assistance to you. Provided"——he grew thoughtful and did not finish his sentence.

"Oh," cried Madame Lenormand, taking Barnett's hands impulsively in hers, "save my husband, and I will give you any reward you care to name."

Barnett shook his head.

"I ask no reward, madame, beyond the privilege of serving you. Never shall it be said that the Barnett Agency descended to base commercialism in accepting a fee for its labors."

At this point a gendarme came running in from the garden with a pair of rubber boots.

"Where did you find those?" asked Béchoux.

"In a garden shed at the back of the grounds of the Villa."

The boots were covered with fresh mud. In this sweltering weather the only moisture on the ground would be along the channel of the stream. Cécile Lenormand gave a sharp exclamation.

"Your husband's?"

She nodded reluctantly.

"Well," said Barnett, "let's go and have a look at the stream—and we ought to take those with us. À bientôt, madame."

Béchoux and Barnett, accompanied by the doctor and the gendarme, walked through the garden and down to the stream. The water was running swiftly over the rocks below.

Béchoux looked unwillingly at the muddy foothold below the broken bridge, and then at his shining new patent leather shoes topped by snowy spats.

"I'll do it!" cried Barnett gallantly, and, seizing a boot from Béchoux, he leapt down, so that he sank ankle-deep in the mud beside the torrent.

"Are there any marks?" asked the doctor eagerly.

"Yes," said Barnett. "And they were made by these boots!"

"A clear case!" said Béchoux. "I need never have brought you along, Barnett, and I'm afraid it's no use your transferring your services to Madame Lenormand. Really, I think you'd better hop back to Paris."

"My dear Béchoux!" said Barnett in tones of shocked surprise. "Go off and leave a client in the lurch? Do you imagine the Barnett Agency shirks what appears to be a losing case?"

"Then you definitely regard Madame Lenormand as your client?"

"Why not?"

He handed up the boot and grovelled a few minutes longer in the mud. Then he clambered up again, somewhat apoplectic of countenance.

"Now," he said briskly, "suppose we visit Mademoiselle Saint-Prix and inspect both the properties prior to consuming beef and wine at the village inn."

"What good can that do? I have my case."

"And I have my own way of working. If you prefer it, I will pursue my course quite independently on behalf of Madame Lenormand, and you needn't see me again until I, too, have my case."

But this course Béchoux viewed with some apprehension, so he and Barnett made their way round by the road to the Saint-Prix house.

On the way there Barnett solemnly handed Béchoux a very grubby sealed envelope.

"Will you please keep that carefully for me?" he said, "and don't let it out of your inner pocket until I ask for it."

"What is it?"

Barnett smiled mysteriously and laid a finger to his nose.

"A valuable diamond, old horse!"

"Idiot!"

At this point, they had arrived at the late professor's house. Here all the blinds were drawn. Barnett observed that the paint was peeling off the walls, and the matting in the passage was worn and old. A down-at-heel servant girl showed them into a small boudoir where they were received by Thérèse Saint-Prix.

She was quite a young woman—a girl in years, but strikingly poised and mature in bearing and appearance, tall and supple. She wore black, with no ornament of any kind. Her smooth black hair, parted in the middle, was drawn off her ears into a knot low on her neck. Her grave, dark eyes searched the faces of the two men—she had already met Béchoux and presumed Barnett to be an assistant.

She sat, very pale, though calm, in a high-backed, carved chair. Only her strong white hands strained at her handkerchief as if there alone her grief found outlet.

Barnett bowed low.

"Accept my profound sympathy, mademoiselle," he murmured. "Your father's death will be felt by all France!"

"Yes," the girl said, in a low voice. "Five years ago he discovered the antiseptic which is now used in every hospital. That brought him renown, though it did not mend our fortunes when we lost our money in Russia." She gave a pathetic little smile.

"How was that?"

"My father was half Russian. He invested everything in his brother's oil-wells near St. Petersburg. Revolutionaries burned the factory and murdered my uncle. After that loss, we lived very modestly. But even in poverty my father was generous. And he would take no money for his discovery. He said his reward was to have been able to help in the great war against disease. When my father died, however, he was on the verge of completing another discovery of a different kind—one that would have brought him wealth as well as fame."

"What was this discovery?"

"A secret process which would have revolutionized the dye industry. But I know scarcely anything about it—my father was secretive in some matters and would not let me help him in his experiments." Again she smiled sadly. "I could only be his housekeeper, never his assistant. And my chief occupation was to interest myself in the garden. Cécile and I used to spend hours planning our flower-beds. She was always so kind, helping me with gifts of plants. She was coming to tea on that afternoon, you know, to advise me about some fruit-trees. Poor Cécile! What will she do?"

"You are aware, mademoiselle," said Béchoux, rather stiffly, as if to recall his presence to her consciousness, "that Louis Lenormand is under arrest? The case is practically complete against him."

She nodded.

"What made Louis Lenormand do such a thing? Can you imagine?" Barnett asked abruptly.

"*If* he did it," said Thérèse gently. "We must remember that nothing is proved yet."

"But what reason can he have had? Well off, prosperous, married to a charming wife——"

"Against the wishes of her family," interposed the girl. "Louis Lenormand was a penniless clerk, and it was by speculating with his wife's money that he became rich. The family all thought that was why he wanted to marry her, though, of course, it was untrue. And Cécile was passionately fond of her husband—she grudged every minute he spent elsewhere. Indeed, I used to wonder if she was not a little jealous of the time he spent with my father in the laboratory. I wondered, too, if she minded his helping my father occasionally with loans of money. But I do wrong if I suggest that Cécile is not all that is generous. Only, where her husband is concerned, if you understand, I have often wondered if she can be quite normal."

Barnett looked distinctly interested, though Béchoux was obviously bored.

"Mademoiselle," said Barnett, "I have a favor to ask of you. May I see the laboratory in which your father worked?"

Without another word she led the way down a passage and through a baize door, which opened into the airy, white building.

The laboratory was in contrast to the house itself. Here all was new and spotless. Phials were ranged in orderly rows along the shelves; clean vessels sparkled on the benches. In all this dazzling whiteness there was but one dark patch—a muddy coat trailing from a stool.

"What's that?" asked Barnett.

"My poor father's coat," said Thérèse. "They carried him in here and removed his coat when they were trying to restore life. But he must have been killed instantaneously."

"And these are all his chemicals?" Barnett indicated the gleaming phials.

"Yes—to think he will never use them again!" She averted her head slightly. "Ah, how my father loved this place; and so, I always thought, did Louis Lenormand. Cécile did not, but that was because she did not understand. She loved flowers, everything beautiful; but science she thought ugly and repellent. Why, I have seen her shake her fist at the laboratory windows when my father and her husband were talking there together."

"Well, mademoiselle, I thank you very much for being so helpful to us in what must be painful and terrible circumstances so far as you are concerned. And I won't hide from you that I have already made one little discovery."

"What's that?" demanded Béchoux.

"Aha, I thought you would want to know. Well, it is that I am on the track of the *motive* for the murder. You have the murderer; I shall soon have the motive. And there we are!"

Then, hastily dissembling his cheerfulness, he took a dignified farewell of Thérèse Saint-Prix, and departed with Béchoux.

At the garden gate they were met by the doctor and the gendarme.

"We've been waiting for you," the former observed. "We have found the instrument of the crime."

The gendarme held up a medium-sized saw.

"Where did you find it?" asked Béchoux eagerly.

"Among some laurel bushes, near the tool-shed where the boots were discovered."

"See," cried Béchoux, turning eagerly to Barnett, "it is plainly marked, 'Villa Eméraude.'"

"Very interesting," observed Barnett. "Béchoux, I feel your case is becoming ever clearer. I almost wish I had never left Paris; it's just as hot here. In fact, I am getting distinctly warm. What about a drink at the local hostelry? I hope you will join us, doctor?" He beamed a comprehensive invitation.

"I shall be delighted to join you and your colleague," answered the doctor.

At the word "colleague," Béchoux smiled wryly. He was wishing pretty heartily that he had never brought Barnett into the case.

The sultry, airless evening was followed by a night of storm, but Barnett slept through the thunderclaps. The next day dawned clear and much cooler.

Béchoux informed his friend that Louis Lenormand was to be examined by the magistrate up at the Saint-Prix house that afternoon.

"I am going to complete the necessary formalities this morning," he announced, sipping his coffee. After a moment he continued, "Won't you change your mind and pop back to Paris?"

"I'm sorry my society bores you so badly," said Barnett sorrowfully, and sought solace in a third cup of chocolate.

"Oh, very well!" Béchoux was inclined to be huffy. He left the inn, and Barnett attacked another soft boiled egg.

When he had finished his breakfast, Jim Barnett spruced himself up and made his way to the Villa Eméraude. Madame Lenormand received him in her sitting-room, and for over an hour he remained talking with her. Towards the end of the interview they moved into Louis Lenormand's study, and Béchoux, coming up the drive, could see through the open window Barnett and Cécile Lenormand bending over an open desk together.

Barnett came out into the hall and greeted his friend as if the Villa Eméraude was his own ancestral hall.

"Welcome, welcome, Béchoux. But I'm afraid you can't see Madame Lenormand. She's feeling overtired already—a little hysterical—and she must rest in view of her ordeal this afternoon. A charming woman; in many ways a delightful woman——" He did not finish, but paused thoughtfully.

Béchoux grunted. "I came up to find you," he said, "to tell you a bit of news."

"What's that?"

"We searched Louis Lenormand, and found on him a note-book in which he made entries of payments made by him during the past six months or so. One of these, dated three weeks ago, was for five thousand francs, paid to 'S,' and against it was written 'The last payment.' Investigation has shown that this amount was paid to Professor Saint-Prix. The case is pretty black against Lenormand, Barnett, and I really should advise you to quit now."

But all Barnett answered was:

"I'm ready for a spot of lunch. Are you?"

The inquiry began at three o'clock. It was held in the narrow dining-room of the Saint-Prix house. Louis Lenormand sat at one end, between two gendarmes, never raising his eyes from the ground. The magistrates and Béchoux conferred together in low tones. Doctor Desportes gazed thoughtfully out of the window.

Barnett ushered in Madame Lenormand. She was very pale and leaned on his arm for support. She took her seat in a low chair, looking all around her with quick, nervous glances. Her husband seemed not to observe her, so sunken was he in dejection.

Then Thérèse Saint-Prix entered the room. Her presence was like a calming influence. She went over to Cécile Lenormand and laid a compassionate hand on her shoulder, but the other started away violently.

Almost immediately the examining magistrate began. He took the medical evidence, which Doctor Desportes gave in even, colorless tones, clearly establishing that the professor had been killed through his fall into the stream.

After this came the questioning of Louis Lenormand.

"Did you take your car out late on Sunday night from the Paris garage?"

"I did."

"Where did you drive?"

The prisoner was silent.

"Answer me!"

"I really forget."

Béchoux gave Barnett a significant look.

"Did you pay Professor Saint-Prix large sums of money from time to time?"

"I did."

"For what reason?"

Louis Lenormand hesitated, and then replied haltingly:

"To assist him in his researches."

Béchoux's pitying contempt was unmistakable.

A small note-book was produced.

"This is yours?"

The prisoner assented.

"Here you have entered various payments made by you. There is one of five thousand francs dated a month ago which says: 'S. *The last payment.*' Was that a check paid to Professor Saint-Prix?"

"It was."

"Won't you tell us why you were being—blackmailed? Perhaps the circumstances——" The magistrate seemed anxious to give Lenormand a chance to defend himself.

"I have nothing to say."

"Is it a fact that Professor Saint-Prix was in the habit of coming to your house for a game of chess on Sunday afternoons?"

"Yes," said the young man sullenly.

"Did you saw through the bridge?"

The prisoner was silent.

"You do not deny that these are your boots?" Béchoux produced them. The prisoner looked slightly startled but made no protest.

"I submit," said Béchoux, "that the case is clear."

"Yes, indeed," said Barnett, "there never was a clearer. As clear as crystal—as a diamond—Béchoux, won't you produce that little envelope I entrusted to your care?"

With a premonition of disaster, Béchoux extracted the rather grubby envelope from his inner pocket.

"Open it!" commanded Barnett.

He did so, and held up—a diamond earring!

Cécile Lenormand gave a little gasp. Her husband started up and then sank back into his chair.

"Can anyone identify this little exhibit of jewelry?" Barnett asked the assembly.

Doctor Desportes looked intensely worried. Poor man, his quiet life was being rudely disturbed!

"Those earrings——" He paused. "They were given to Madame Lenormand by her husband not very long ago!"

"Is that so?" Béchoux asked of Louis Lenormand.

The latter nodded.

Cécile had bowed her head in her hands. Thérèse reached out a pitying hand to her, but she shook it off wildly.

"You have seen these earrings," pursued Barnett, "but you can't guess where I found one of them. Inspector Béchoux will tell you, though. In the mud by the stream, at the point where the body of Professor Saint-Prix was found lying dead!"

"Can you tell us, madame," inquired the magistrate of Cécile Lenormand, "whether you were wearing those earrings on Sunday afternoon?"

Looking up, the young woman shook her head.

"I can't—remember—when I last wore them!" she said in a confused manner.

"You must forgive my asking you, madame, but you must tell us now whether you left the Villa at any time during Saturday night."

There was the merest hint of menace in the smooth tones. Louis Lenormand's mouth twitched painfully.

"I—I——" She looked from one face to another of those gathered in the room. "Why, I believe I did. It was so hot.... I went out into the garden for a little...."

"Was this before you retired for the night?"

"Yes—no—not exactly. I had gone to my room, but I had not undressed. I had told my maid to go to bed. Then I felt oppressed by the heat and went out into the garden through the French window of my boudoir."

"So that no one heard you come or go?"

"No one, monsieur."

"And, on Sunday afternoon, you were going to tea with Mademoiselle Saint-Prix?"

"Yes."

"At four o'clock?"

"That's so——"

Thérèse Saint-Prix's voice here interrupted gently, like a low-toned bell.

"Don't you remember, Cécile, the arrangement was that you should come over soon after three to me, but that if you did not arrive by four, I was to come up to the Villa? Why, I was just getting ready to come when—when *it* happened. You see," she turned to address the magistrate, "we were going to make gardening plans together, but just lately Cécile hasn't been feeling too well, and she thought it possible that she might not feel up to walking about the garden in the hot sun. So I was quite prepared for her to stay resting in her boudoir that afternoon, and then we would have had tea together there."

"Is that true, madame?" asked the magistrate of Cécile Lenormand.

"I—I can't remember. Perhaps that was the arrangement."

"But—but——" Béchoux was stammering under the force of his discovery—"if you, mademoiselle, had been just a few minutes quicker in getting ready to go up to the Villa, you might yourself have been killed!"

"The question that presents itself," said Barnett, in a level voice, "is— for whom was the trap laid? Did Louis Lenormand lay it to kill Professor Saint-Prix? We must remember that the old professor was absent-minded, and was in the custom of going to play chess with his neighbor on Sunday afternoon. Or, was the attack directed by Louis Lenormand against his own wife? Or against Mademoiselle Saint-Prix?"

"Or," said Béchoux, annoyed to find Barnett calmly taking the floor, "did Madame Lenormand saw through the bridge because she guessed Professor Saint-Prix would be coming that way? Remember what Mademoiselle Saint-Prix has told us——"

Thérèse Saint-Prix was covered with confusion.

"I never meant you to take it that way," she cried.

"Why, I only said Cécile sometimes appeared a little jealous of her husband's intimacy with my poor father. But that was nothing! Poor darling, she was always jealous where Louis—Monsieur Lenormand—was concerned. Why, she even at one time——" She broke off and was silent.

"She even what, mademoiselle?" asked the magistrate.

"Oh, it's too silly. But at one time I used to wonder if she were not a little jealous of *me*! I was giving Monsieur Lenormand lessons in Russian—a language he was eager to learn—and so we were naturally together a good deal. I even wondered if Cécile could be—could be spying on us—she seemed so queer. But please don't misunderstand me, I'm not suggesting a thing against her."

"But mademoiselle is right," said Barnett gravely. "Madame Lenormand had the most odd ideas concerning her husband and mademoiselle—almost unbelievable. She imagined—I ask you!—that Mademoiselle Saint-Prix had almost forced Monsieur Lenormand into having Russian lessons, in the hope that she might thereby succeed in teaching him something besides Russian! She had the absurd hallucination that she once saw her husband kissing you, mademoiselle, in the little summer-house at the bottom of the garden. And yet, and this is the most unbelievable part of all, she never really doubted her husband—she believed that, like so many men, he was capable of being superficially attracted without being guilty of any serious infidelity. A trusting woman, one would say. But her clemency hardly extended to her supposed rival.

"Now, on Sunday afternoon a woman telephoned from Beauvray to Louis Lenormand at his mother's flat and told him something terrible—so terrible, in fact, as to bring him racing home in his car to try and avert disaster. But he was too late. The tragedy had occurred. Only, it was something quite different from what he had feared! To-day you have before you a woman telling a vague, unsubstantiated story of having wandered about on Saturday night in her garden—of having, *perhaps*, asked her friend to come to tea instead of going to tea with her. And, on the other hand, you must picture to yourselves a woman mad with jealousy and fury—a woman telephoning in words of ice-cold rage—'She shall no longer come between us —she and she alone is the obstacle to our love—it is because of her that you have turned a deaf ear to my entreaties, but soon, soon the obstacle will be removed!'

"Gentlemen, which story are you going to believe?"

"There can be but one answer to that," observed the magistrate, "if you have proof of what you say. And much is explained if Cécile Lenormand did indeed telephone to her husband in Paris that afternoon!"

"Did I say that Cécile Lenormand telephoned?" asked Barnett, looking most surprised. "But that would be quite contrary to my own belief—and to the truth!"

"Then what on earth do you mean?"

"Exactly what I say. The telephone call from Beauvray to Paris was made by a woman maddened by jealousy and frustration, by a desire to annihilate her rival in Louis Lenormand's affections——"

"But that woman is Cécile Lenormand."

"Not a bit of it! I can assure you she had nothing whatever to do with the telephone call."

"Then whom are you accusing?"

"The other woman!"

"But there were only two—Cécile Lenormand and Thérèse Saint-Prix."

"Precisely, and since I am *not* accusing Cécile Lenormand, that means that I *do* accuse...."

Barnett left the sentence unfinished. There was a horrified silence. Here was a direct and totally unforeseen accusation! Thérèse Saint-Prix, who was at this moment standing near the window, hesitated for a long moment, pale and trembling. Suddenly she sprang over the low balcony and down into the garden.

The doctor and a gendarme made to pursue her, but found themselves in collision with Barnett, who was barring the way. The gendarme protested hotly:

"But we shall have her escaping!"

"I think not," said Barnett.

"You're right," said the doctor, appalled, "but I fear something else— something ghastly!... Yes, look, look! She's running towards the stream ... towards the bridge where her father was killed."

"What next?" came from Barnett with terrible calm.

He stood aside. The doctor and the gendarme were out of the window like lightning, and he closed it behind them. Then, turning to the magistrate, he said:

"Do you understand the whole business now, monsieur? Is it quite clear to you? It was Thérèse Saint-Prix who, after trying vainly to rouse the passion of Louis Lenormand beyond the passing fancy of a flirtation—Thérèse Saint-Prix who, starved for years of all enjoyment and luxury, was suddenly blinded by hatred of Cécile Lenormand. She was too proud to believe that Louis Lenormand genuinely did not want her love and was devoted to his wife. She thought that if once Cécile Lenormand were out of the way, she would come into her own. So she planned the appalling, cold-blooded murder of her rival, and—compassed the death of her own father! In the night she sawed through the bridge—there was no one to see her. So blinded was

91

she by her passions that next day, just before the tragedy would occur, she telephoned to Louis Lenormand to tell him what she had done.

"Confronted by the utterly unexpected result of her strategy, she immediately planned to throw the guilt on to Cécile Lenormand and so at one stroke save herself and get her rival out of the way. It was with this in view that she stole one of Cécile's earrings and dropped it on Sunday night into the ditch, and then told her tale of Cécile having been jealous of the old professor. Then, here in this room, she was struck with a more plausible idea altogether—she tried to get us all to believe that the bridge had been sawed through with the object of killing *her* and not her father at all!"

"How do you account for the boots and the saw?" asked the magistrate.

"The Lenormands and the Saint-Prix shared a tool-shed, their garden implements were used in common."

"How do you know all about Thérèse Saint-Prix?" asked Lenormand, speaking for the first time.

"I helped him to find out," said Cécile swiftly. "My dear, I realized all along how you were placed in the matter, but my pride kept me from speaking to you. I was afraid you would think I was being jealous, and trying to find something to throw in your face because my parents tried to prevent our marriage."

"Then you forgive me?"

For answer she ran across the room to her husband, and her arms went round his neck.

"But," objected the magistrate, "that entry in the note-book of 'the last payment'—what did that mean?"

"Merely," said Barnett, "that Professor Saint-Prix had told Louis Lenormand that this was the last loan he would need, as his discovery was on the verge of completion."

"And that discovery——"

"Was something which would have revolutionized the dye industry. Doubtless he was going eagerly up to the Villa Eméraude to show it to his friend, and the stream washed it out of his dying grasp. What a loss!"

"And where *did* Monsieur Lenormand drive that night?"

"He shall tell us himself."

"I drove," said the erstwhile prisoner, "into the country a little way. I honestly could not say exactly where. I did so because it was very hot and I couldn't sleep. But no one could prove the truth of what I say."

At this point the gendarme came back, rather pale.

Barnett signed to him to speak.

"She is dead!" he faltered. "She threw herself down—there, where the professor was killed! The doctor sent me to tell you."

The magistrate looked grave.

"Perhaps, after all, it is for the best," he said. "But for you, monsieur," he turned to Barnett, "there might have been a grave miscarriage of justice."

Béchoux stood awkwardly silent.

"Come, Béchoux," said Barnett, clapping him on the shoulder, "let's be off and pack our things. I want to be back in the *rue Laborde* tonight."

"Well," said Béchoux when they were alone together again, "I admit that I do not see how you reconstructed the case so quickly."

"Quite simple, my dear Béchoux—like all my little *coups*. What faith that woman had in her husband!"

For a moment he was silent in admiration of his client.

"Still," said Béchoux, "brilliant as you were, I fail to see where you get anything out of this for yourself!"

Barnett's gaze grew dreamy.

"That was a beautiful laboratory of the professor's," he said. "By the way, Béchoux, do you happen to know the address of the biggest dye concern in the country? I may be paying them a call in the near future!"

Béchoux gave a curious gasp, rather like a slowly expiring balloon.

"Done me again!" he breathed. "Stolen the paper—the formula of the secret process...."

Jim Barnett was moved to injured protest.

"Dear old chap," he observed, "when it's a question of rendering a service to one's fellow-men and to one's country, what *you* designate as theft becomes the sheerest heroism. It is the highest manifestation of duty's sacred fire, blazing within the breast of mere man." He thumped himself significantly on the chest. "And personally, when duty calls, you will always find me ready, aye ready. Got that, Béchoux?"

But Béchoux was sunk in gloom.

"I wonder," Barnett mused, "what they will call the new process? I think a suitable name might be—but there, I won't bore you with my reflections, Béchoux. Only I can't help feeling it would be rather touching to take out a patent in the name of—Lupin!"

CHAPTER VIII

THE FATAL MIRACLE

Shortly after the suicide of Thérèse Saint-Prix, Inspector Béchoux, primed with official information, was hastily despatched from police headquarters on the mission of solving the Old Dungeon mystery. He left Paris on an evening train and spent the night at Guéret in central France. Next day he took a car on to the village of Mazurech, where his first move was to visit the château—a vast, rambling structure, of great age, built on a promontory in a loop of the river Creuse. He found the owner, Monsieur Georges Cazévon, in residence.

Georges Cazévon was a rich manufacturer of about forty—handsome in a florid style, and not without a certain animal attraction. He had a bluff, hearty manner which commanded the respect of the neighborhood. Thanks to influence, he was chairman of the County Council and a person of considerable importance. Since the Old Dungeon was on his estate, he was eager to take Béchoux there himself immediately.

They walked across the great park with its fine chestnuts, and came to a ruined tower, all that was left of the ancient feudal castle of Mazurech. This tower soared skywards right from the bottom of the canyon where the Creuse crawled like a wounded snake along its rock-strewn bed.

The opposite bank of the river was the property of the d'Alescar family, and on it, about forty yards away from where Béchoux stood with Cazévon, rose a rubble wall, glistening with moisture and forming a kind of dam. Higher up it was surmounted by a shady terrace with a balustrade along it, forming the end of a garden alley. It was a wild, forlorn spot. Here it was that, on a morning ten days before, the young Comte Jean d'Alescar had been found lying dead on a great rock. The body apparently had no injuries other than those due to the ghastly fall. There was a broken branch hanging down the trunk of one of the trees on the terrace. It was easy to reconstruct the tragedy—the young Comte had climbed out along the branch, it had snapped beneath his weight, and he had fallen into the river. A clear case of death by misadventure. There had been no hesitation in bringing in the verdict.

"But what on earth was the young Comte doing climbing that tree?" Béchoux wanted to know.

Georges Cazévon was ready with the answer.

"He wanted to get a really close view from above of this dungeon. The old castle is the cradle of the d'Alescar family, who lorded it here in feudal times." He added immediately: "I shan't say anything more, inspector. You know that you have been sent here at my urgent request. The trouble is that ugly rumors have got about and I am being attacked on all sides. That's got to stop. So please make the fullest investigations and question everyone. It is especially important that you should call on Mademoiselle d'Alescar, the young Comte's sister, and the last surviving member of the family. Look me up again before you leave Mazurech."

Béchoux went about his work quickly. He explored round the foot of the tower and then entered the inner court which was now a mass of fallen masonry caused by the collapse of stairs and flooring. He then made his way back into Mazurech, picking up stray bits of information from the inhabitants. He called on the priest and on the mayor, and lunched at the inn.

At two o'clock that afternoon, Béchoux stood in the narrow garden which ran down to the terrace and was bisected by a small building of farmhouse type, called the Manor—a nondescript structure in bad repair. An old servant took his card into Mademoiselle d'Alescar and he was at once shown into a low, plainly furnished room where he found the object of his call in conversation with a man.

Both rose at his entrance, and, as the man turned towards him, Béchoux recognized—Jim Barnett!

"Ah, you've come at last!" exclaimed Barnett joyously and held out his hand. "When I read in my morning paper that you were cruising Creuse-ward I leapt into my car and hastened to the scene of action so that I might be ready at your service. In fact, I was here waiting for you! Mademoiselle, may I introduce Inspector Béchoux, who has been put in charge of the case by headquarters. With Béchoux at the helm you need fear nothing. Probably by now he has the whole thing cut and dried. Béchoux puts the sleuth in sleuthing—burglars frighten their young with tales of Bogey Béchoux. Let him speak for himself!"

But Béchoux uttered not a word. He was flabbergasted. Barnett's presence—the last thing he had either expected or desired—floored him completely. It was a case of Barnett morning, noon, and night. Barnett popping up like a jack-in-the-box on every possible—and impossible—occasion. Every time that fate brought the two together, Béchoux found himself perforce submitting to Barnett's accursed coöperation. And where Jim Barnett helped others, he was always careful to help himself. His hand went out to his fellow-men, but never drew back empty!

In truth, there was little enough Béchoux could say anyway, for he was still quite at sea and had found no clue in the Old Dungeon mystery—if mystery it should prove.

As he remained silent, Barnett spoke again:

"The position, mademoiselle, is this: Inspector Béchoux, having by this time, doubtless, examined the evidence and made up his own mind, is here to ask if you will be so kind as to confirm the results of the inquiries he has already made. Since we ourselves have only had the briefest of conversation so far, would you be good enough to tell us all you know about the terrible tragedy which resulted in the death of your brother, Comte d'Alescar?"

Elizabeth d'Alescar was a tall girl, classically beautiful, her pallor accentuated by her mourning. She kept her face turned away into the shadow so that the two men saw only her delicate profile. It was with a visible effort that she restrained her grief. She answered without hesitation:

"I would rather have said nothing, have accused no one. But since it is my painful duty to reveal all I know to you, I am ready to speak."

It was Barnett who authoritatively usurped the law's prerogative.

"My friend, Inspector Béchoux, would like to know the exact time at which you last saw your brother alive."

"At ten o'clock at night. We had dined together—our usual light-hearted meal. I was very, very fond of Jean; he was several years younger than myself, and I had practically brought him up from when he was quite a little boy. We were always the best of friends, and happy in each other's company."

"He went out during the night?"

"He left the house a little before dawn, towards half-past three in the morning. Our old servant heard him go."

"Did you know where he was going?"

"He had told me the day before that he was going to fish from the terrace. Fishing was one of his favorite occupations."

"Then there is nothing you can tell us about the time elapsing between half-past three and the discovery of your brother's body?"

"Yes, there is." She paused. "At a quarter past six I heard a shot!"

"Oh, yes. Several people heard it. But it's quite possible it was only a poacher."

"That was what I thought at the time. But somehow I felt anxious, so at last I got out of bed and dressed. When I reached the terrace I saw men from the village on the opposite bank of the river. They were carrying my poor brother up to the grounds of the Château, because it was too steep to get the body up the other side."

"Then you are surely of opinion that the shot could not have been in any way connected with what happened to your brother? Otherwise the inquest would have revealed a bullet wound, which, of course, it did not."

Seeing Mademoiselle d'Alescar's hesitation, Barnett pressed home his question.

"Won't you answer me?"

The girl's hands clenched at her sides.

"Whatever actually happened, I only know that I am perfectly certain in my own mind that there *is* some connection."

"What makes you think that?"

"Well, to begin with, there is no other possible explanation."

"An accident...."

She shook her head, smiling sadly.

"Oh, no. Jean was extraordinarily agile, and he had also plenty of good sense and caution. He would never have trusted himself to that branch. Why, it was obviously much too slender to bear his weight."

"But you admit that it was broken."

"There is nothing to prove that it was broken by him and on that particular night."

"Then, mademoiselle, it is your honest belief that a crime has been committed?"

She nodded gravely.

"You have even gone so far as to accuse a certain person by name and in the presence of witnesses?"

Again she nodded.

"What grounds have you for making this assertion? Is there any definite proof pointing to someone's guilt? That is what Inspector Béchoux is anxious to know."

For a few moments Elizabeth was lost in reflection. They could see that it distressed her to recall such dreadful memories. But she made a valiant effort and said:

"I will tell you everything. But to do so, I must go back to something that happened twenty-four years ago. It was then that my father lost all his money in a bank failure. He found himself ruined, but he told no one. His creditors were paid. Of course, it was common knowledge that he had lost a large part of his fortune, but no one guessed that the whole of it had been engulfed. What actually happened was that my father threw himself on the mercy of a rich manufacturer in Guéret. This man lent him two hundred thousand francs on one condition only—that the Château, the estate, and all the Mazurech acres should become his property if the loan were not repaid within five years."

"That manufacturer was Georges Cazévon's father, wasn't he?"

"Yes," she said, a note of hatred in her voice.

"Was he anxious to own the Château?"

"Very anxious indeed. He had tried to buy it several times. Well, exactly four years and eleven months later, my father died of cerebral congestion. It came on rapidly, and towards the close of his life he was obviously troubled and preoccupied with something of which we knew nothing. Immediately after his death, Georges Cazévon told us about the loan he had made my father, and warned my uncle, who was looking after us, that we had just one month in which to discharge our debt. He had absolute proof of his claim, such proof as no lawyer could dispute. My father left nothing. Jean and I were driven out of our home and were taken in by our uncle, who lived in this very house, and was himself far from wealthy. He died very soon after, and so did old Monsieur Cazévon."

Béchoux and Barnett had listened to her attentively. Now Barnett spoke on behalf of his friend:

"My friend the inspector doesn't quite see how all this links up with the events of the present day."

Mademoiselle d'Alescar gave Béchoux a glance of slightly contemptuous surprise and continued, without answering:

"So Jean and I lived alone here on this little manor, right in front of the Dungeon and the Château that had always belonged to our family. This caused Jean a sorrow which grew with the years, and intensified as his intelligence developed and he grew towards manhood. It grieved and hurt him to feel that he had lost his heritage and been driven from what he considered his rightful domain. In all his work and play he made time to devote whole days to delving in the family archives, and reading up our history and genealogy. Then, one day, he found among these books a ledger in which our father had kept his accounts during the latter years of his life, showing the money he had saved by exercising the strictest economy and by several successful real estate deals. There were also bank receipts. I went to the bank that had issued them and learned that our father, a week before his death, had withdrawn his entire deposit—two hundred banknotes of a thousand francs each!"

"The exact amount," said Barnett, "which he was due to pay in a few weeks' time. Then why did he put off paying it?"

"I have no idea."

"Therefore you think he must have put the money in a safe place somewhere?" He paused, and twiddled his monocle thoughtfully. "Somewhere—ah, but where?"

Elizabeth d'Alescar produced the ledger of which she had spoken and showed it to Barnett and Béchoux.

"It is here that we must look for the answer to that question," she said, turning to the last page, on which was sketched a diagram representing three-quarters of a circle, to which was added, at the right side, a semicircle of shorter radius. This semicircle was barred by four lines, between two of which was a small cross. All the lines in the diagram had been drawn first in pencil and then gone over in ink.

"What's all this mean?" asked Barnett.

"It took us a long time to understand it," replied Elizabeth. "At last, poor Jean guessed one day that the diagram represented an accurate plan of the Old Dungeon, reduced to its outside lines. It is on that exact plan, on the unequal parts of two circles connected with each other. The four lines indicate four embrasures."

"And the cross," finished Barnett, "indicates the place where the Comte d'Alescar hid his two hundred thousand francs to await the day of repayment."

"Yes," said the girl, with conviction.

Barnett thought it over, took another look at the map and finally remarked:

"It's quite probable. The Comte d'Alescar would, of course, have been sure to take the precaution of leaving some clue to the hiding-place, and his sudden death prevented his passing on the secret. But surely, all you had to do on finding this was to tell Monsieur Cazévon's son and ask his permission to——"

"To climb to the top of the tower! That is just what we immediately did. Georges Cazévon, although we were not on the best of terms with him, was quite pleasant about it. But how could any human being get to the top of that tower? The stairs had fallen in fifteen years before. All the stones are loose. The top is crumbling. No ladder—no ladders even—could ever have reached high enough. The Dungeon battlements are over ninety feet above the ground. And it was quite out of the question to scale the wall. We discussed the whole problem and drew up plans for several months, but it all ended in——"

She broke off, blushing hotly.

"A quarrel!" Barnett finished for her. "Georges Cazévon fell in love with you and asked you to marry him. You refused him. He tried to force you to his will. You broke off all intercourse with him, and Jean d'Alescar was no longer allowed to set foot on Mazurech land."

"That is exactly what did happen," the girl said. "But my brother would not give up. He simply had to have that money. He wanted it to buy back part of our estate or to give me a *dot* which would set me free to marry as I chose. Very soon the idea obsessed him. He spent his days in front of the tower. He was always staring up at the inaccessible battlements. He imag-

99

ined a thousand schemes for getting up there. He practiced until he was a skilled archer, and then, from daybreak, he would stand there shooting arrows on long strings, hoping that one of them would fall in such a way that a rope could be tied to the string and pulled up to the top of the tower. He even had sixty yards of rope all ready for the attempt. Everything he tried was hopeless, and his failure plunged him into melancholy and despair. On the very day before he died he said to me: 'The only reason I go on trying is that I am certain to succeed in the end. Fate will be in my favor. There will be a miracle—I am sure of it—a miracle! That is what I pray for and what I confidently expect.' Poor Jean, he never had his miracle!"

Barnett put another question.

"Then you believe that his death occurred while he was making yet another attempt?"

Seeing that she assented, he continued:

"Is the rope no longer where he kept it?"

"Yes, it is."

"Then what proof have you?"

"That shot! Georges Cazévon must have caught my brother in his attempt and fired."

"Good God!" cried Barnett. "You believe Georges Cazévon is capable of doing such a thing?"

"I do. He is very impulsive. He controls himself as a rule, but he might easily be led into violence—or even into crime."

"But why should he have fired? To rob your brother of the money he had recovered?"

"That I cannot say," said Mademoiselle d'Alescar. "Nor do I know how the murder could have been committed, since poor Jean's dead body showed no trace of a bullet wound. But I am absolutely firm in my belief."

"Quite so, but you must admit that your belief is based on intuition rather than on the known facts," observed Barnett. "And I think I ought to tell you that in a court of law, intuition is not enough. I'm sure Béchoux will agree with me, it's quite on the cards that Georges Cazévon will be so furious at your accusing him that he will sue you for libel."

Mademoiselle d'Alescar rose from her chair.

"That would matter very little to me," she said. "I have not made this accusation to avenge my brother, for to punish the criminal would not restore Jean to life. I am merely stating what I believe to be the truth. If Georges Cazévon likes to sue me, he is perfectly free to do so and my defence will simply be what my conscience moves me to say."

She was silent for a moment, and then added:

"But you can rely on his keeping quiet, gentlemen. I don't think there is much chance of his bringing any action against me!"

The interview was at an end. Jim Barnett did not attempt to engage the girl in further conversation. Mademoiselle d'Alescar knew her own mind, and no one would be able to intimidate her or upset her evidence in the least.

"Mademoiselle," said Barnett, "we apologize for this intrusion, but we were obliged to trouble you in order to get at the truth of this tragic affair. You may be sure Inspector Béchoux will make the right deductions from all that you have said and act accordingly."

He bowed and took his leave. Béchoux bowed likewise, and followed him into the courtyard.

Once they were out of the house, the inspector, who had not spoken during the interview, continued silent, partly in protest against Barnett's interference in the case, and partly because he was totally bewildered by the turn events were taking. His taciturnity only encouraged the loquacious Barnett.

"Yes, yes, Béchoux," he said reflectively, "I can easily understand your being puzzled. It's a matter for deep thought. The lady's statement had a good deal in it, but it was compounded of such a mixture of the possible with the impossible, the rational with the fantastic, that it needs careful sifting if we are to make use of it. For instance, on the face of it, young d'Alescar's actions seem pure fantasy. If the unlucky youth got to the top of the tower—and, contrary to your own private belief, I rather think he *did* get there—then it was due to that unimaginable miracle he had hoped and prayed for—a miracle whose nature we are as yet unable to conceive.

"The problem we are up against is—how could the boy, within the space of two hours, invent a means of climbing the tower, put his scheme into execution, and climb down again, only to be hurled into the abyss by a bullet … which did not hit him! That's the culminating impossibility, that he went to his death through a shot which never touched him—*that* seems to me to have been a miracle from hell!"

Barnett and Béchoux met again that evening at the inn, but dined apart. During the next two days they only saw each other at mealtimes. Béchoux was busy making investigations and inquiries throughout the neighborhood. Barnett, like one of the lilies of the field, took root on a grassy slope some way beyond the terrace, from which spot he had a good view of the Old Dungeon and the river Creuse. He confined his activities to fishing, smoking, and reflection. The heart of a mystery is to be plucked out by sheer divination rather than by fevered probing. So Barnett sat there, angling with his rod for the fish in the river, and with his mind for the nature of the miracle with which Fate had favored Jean d'Alescar.

On the third day, however, he bestirred himself and went off to Guéret in the manner of a man with a definite object. And the day after that he ran into Béchoux, who told him that he had now finished his investigation.

"So have I," said Barnett. "If you're going back to Paris, I'll give you a lift in my car."

"Thanks," said Béchoux. "In about half an hour I am going up to see Monsieur Cazévon."

"Right, I'll meet you at the Château," said Barnett. "I'm fed to the teeth with this place, aren't you?"

He paid his bill at the inn, and drove to the gates of the Château. Leaving his car in the road, he strolled through the park, and when he got to the house presented his card. Underneath his own name he had written the words: "*Working in collaboration with Inspector Béchoux.*"

He was shown into a vast hall, which spread over the ground floor of an entire wing. Stags' heads looked down from the walls, which were hung with weapons and trophies of every description. Here he was joined by Georges Cazévon.

"My colleague, Inspector Béchoux," said Barnett, "is to meet me here. We have been working together on the case, and we are today returning to Paris."

"And what opinion has Inspector Béchoux formed as a result of his investigation?" asked Georges Cazévon, a shade eagerly.

"Oh, he has definitely made up his mind that there is nothing, absolutely nothing to justify any fresh theory of the case. He is satisfied that the rumors set afloat are quite groundless."

"And Mademoiselle d'Alescar?"

Barnett shrugged his shoulders.

"According to Inspector Béchoux her mind is almost unhinged by her bereavement, so that no reliance can be placed on anything she says at present."

"And you agree with Inspector Béchoux?"

"I?" Barnett raised his eyes and lowered them, his whole attitude one of abject humility. "I am nothing but a humble assistant. I have no views of my own at all!"

He began wandering aimlessly about the hall, looking at the glass cases full of rifles and shotguns. These exhibits seemed to interest him considerably.

"A fine collection, aren't they?" said Georges Cazévon at his elbow.

"Magnificent!"

"Are you an enthusiast?"

"I have a great admiration for good marksmanship. I see by these cups and certificates that you must be a remarkable shot. Let's see—*Disciples de Saint Hubert*, Creuse Sporting Club—oh, yes, that's what they were telling me about you yesterday when I was in Guéret."

"Is the case much talked about at Guéret?"

"Oh, very little. But the accuracy of your shooting is proverbial among the townsfolk!"

Barnett took up a gun, balancing it casually in his hands.

"Careful!" said Cazévon sharply. "That's a service rifle. It's loaded."

"Really?" observed Barnett with polite interest. "Is that in case of burglars?"

Cazévon smiled. "I really keep it handy for poachers. I should never shoot to kill, though. A broken leg would be all I should aim for!"

"And would you shoot from one of these windows?"

"Oh, poachers don't come so close to the Château!"

"That almost seems a pity," said Barnett thoughtfully, and opened a very narrow window—almost a loophole—which shed a ray of light into one corner of the hall.

"Fancy that now!" he exclaimed. "Looking through the trees, one can see a section of the Old Dungeon—right across the park. Isn't that the portion of the ruin which overlooks the river, Monsieur Cazévon?"

"Just about, I should say."

"Why, yes, it is!" cried Barnett excitedly. "I recognize that tuft of flowers growing between two stones. Isn't the air wonderfully clear? Can you see that yellow flower, looking along the bore?"

He had raised the gun to his shoulder as he spoke, and without hesitating a moment, he fired. The yellow flower disappeared, while a puff of smoke hung in the still air.

Georges Cazévon made a gesture of annoyance. His displeasure was manifest. This "humble assistant" was an incredibly skilled marksman, and, anyway, it was cool cheek his letting off a gun like that in the house!

"I believe your servants are at the other end of the Château?" said Barnett. "Then they won't have heard the noise I made. But I'm sorry I did that —it must have startled Mademoiselle d'Alescar, the sound being so painfully associated for her with the memory——" He broke off.

Georges Cazévon smiled sardonically.

"Then does Mademoiselle d'Alescar still believe there is some connection between the shot that was heard that morning and her brother's death?"

Barnett nodded.

"I wonder where she got the idea?"

"Where I got it myself a minute ago. It's a curiously vivid picture—the unknown watcher in ambush at this window, while Jean d'Alescar was hanging on half-way down the Dungeon wall!"

"But d'Alescar died of a fall!" protested Cazévon.

"Quite so," said Barnett, with deadly calm, "of a fall. And the reason for his fall was, of course, the sudden crumbling of some projection or shelf to which he was clinging with both hands at the time!"

Cazévon scowled at the urbane Barnett.

"I didn't know," he said, "that Mademoiselle d'Alescar had been so—so definite in her statements to people. Why, this constitutes a direct accusation!"

"Yes, a—direct—accusation," repeated Barnett slowly, so that the words seemed to hang in the air as the smoke from the gun had done a few moments before.

Cazévon stared at him. The calm self-assurance and decisive manner of this "humble assistant" rather astonished him. He even began to wonder if this detective might not have come to the Château in the rôle of aggressor. For the conversation, begun so casually and conventionally, was now rapidly turning into an attack on Cazévon himself!

He sat down rather heavily, and asked:

"Why, according to Mademoiselle d'Alescar, was her brother climbing that wall?"

"To recover the two hundred thousand francs which the old Comte d'Alescar hid in the place which is marked with a cross on the map you have been shown."

"But I never for a moment believed in that yarn," exclaimed Cazévon. "Even presuming that the Comte d'Alescar had managed to raise such a sum, why should he have concealed it instead of immediately handing it over to my father?"

"Quite a valid objection," admitted Barnett. "Unless the hidden treasure happened not to be a sum of money at all!"

"But what else could it be?"

"That I don't know. We shall have to use our imaginations a bit."

Georges Cazévon made a movement of impatience.

"You can be quite sure that Elizabeth d'Alescar and her brother long ago exhausted the possible alternatives!"

"How do you know? They are not professionals like myself."

"Even a hypersensitized intelligence," sneered Cazévon, "cannot evolve something from nothing!"

"Yes, it can—sometimes! For example, do you know a man called Gréaume, who is the Guéret newsagent, and was at one time an accountant in your factory?"

"Certainly I know him. A very worthy fellow."

"Well, Gréaume is prepared to swear that Jean d'Alescar's father called on your own father the very next day after he had drawn his two hundred thousand francs from the bank."

"Well?" snapped Cazévon.

"Isn't it only logical to suppose that the money was handed over to your father on that occasion, and that it was *the receipt* which was temporarily concealed in some cranny of the Dungeon?"

Georges Cazévon gave a sudden start, then controlled himself.

"Mr.—uh—Barnett, do you realize what you are insinuating? It's an insult to my father's memory!"

"An insult! I don't follow you!" said Barnett innocently.

"If my father had received that money he would most certainly have acknowledged the fact."

"Why should he? He was under no obligation to tell his neighbors that some one had paid him back a private loan!"

Georges Cazévon's fist came down with a bang on his desk.

"But if that money had been paid him, how do you explain that a fortnight later, just a few days after his former debtor's death, he was taking possession of the Mazurech estate?"

"Yet that is exactly what he did!"

"You must be crazy! There's absolutely no ground for suggesting such a thing. Even granting that my father was capable of demanding to be paid what he had already received, he would never have done it, because he would have known that the receipt could be produced!"

"Perhaps he knew," suggested Barnett diffidently, "that its existence was a secret and that the heirs were in ignorance of both loan and repayment. And since he had set his heart on owning this place and had, so they tell me, sworn he would get it, he was tempted and fell."

"But no one would hide a receipt away where it could never be found."

"Remember that the old Comte died of cerebral congestion. During his last days he was very queer. His mind reasoned imperfectly. He was ashamed of having borrowed that money. He was ashamed of the receipt, yet dared not destroy it. So he evolved a tortuous manner of concealment, with an equally tortuous clew."

Gradually Barnett was putting a completely different complexion on the whole case. Georges Cazévon's father was now appearing in the light of a rogue and blackguard. Cazévon himself, pale and shaking, stood with clenched fists, impotent with fear and rage, glaring at the immovable Barnett. The audacity of this "underling" completely unnerved him.

"I protest!" he stammered. "You have no right to jump to these—these abominable conclusions!"

"Believe me," said Barnett, "I never leap before I look. All my allegations are founded on fact."

Georges Cazévon darted a hunted look over his shoulder. He felt as if some unseen enemy were closing in on him. In a high, unnatural voice he cried:

"Lies! all lies! You have no proof. To prove that my father ever did such a thing you would—why, you would have to go and look for evidence at the top of the Old Dungeon!"

"Well," contested Barnett, "Jean d'Alescar managed to get there, didn't he?"

"He didn't! I tell you he didn't! I tell you it's impossible to scale a ninety-foot tower all in two hours. It's beyond human power!"

"All the same, Jean d'Alescar accomplished this—impossibility," pursued Barnett doggedly.

"But how?" asked Georges Cazévon, on a note of sheer exasperation. "Do you expect me to believe he went up on a witch's broomstick?"

"Not that," said Barnett gently. "He used a rope!"

Cazévon laughed long and loud, but quite unmirthfully.

"A rope? You're crazy. Of course, I often saw the boy shooting his arrows in the vain hope that one day his rope would catch hold. Poor devil! Miracles like that never happen nowadays. And anyway, two hours! Oh, it's out of the question. Besides, the rope would have been found hanging from the tower, or lying on the rocks of the Creuse after the tragedy. Whereas I am told it is at the Manor."

With unshakable calm Barnett rejoined:

"Quite. But it wasn't that rope he used, you see."

"Then what rope *did* he use?" asked Cazévon, turning a gulp into a laugh. "You can't expect me to take all this seriously, you know. The Comte Jean d'Alescar, carrying the magic rope, came out on to the terrace of his garden at daybreak. He muttered the one word 'Abracadabra,' and lo! his rope uncoiled and rose to the top of the tower, so that he might promptly ascend. The good old Indian rope-trick—retired colonels write to the papers every day and solemnly aver it's a miracle!"

"And yet you, too, monsieur," said Barnett, "are driven to conjure up a miracle;—just like Jean d'Alescar—and like myself. There is no other explanation, of course. But the miracle was the opposite of what you imagine —it did not work from bottom to top, as would seem more usual and probable, but from top to bottom!"

Cazévon made a feeble attempt to joke.

"A kind Providence, eh, throwing a life-line to help a struggling mortal?"

"Why call Providence into it?" asked Barnett. "No need for that. This miracle was merely one of those which Chance may perform at any time nowadays."

"Chance?"

"Remember that Chance knows no impossibilities. Chance is the unknown factor—Chance the disturber, the malicious, capricious visitant, swooping to make fantastic moves on the chessboard of human existence, forever proving the old platitude that truth is stranger than fiction! Chance is today the great worker of miracles. And the miracle I have in mind is not so wonderful, really, in an age when meteors are not the only bolts from the blue, so to speak."

"Do the skies rain ropes?" asked Cazévon sardonically.

"Certainly, ropes among other things. The ocean-bed is strewn with things dropped overboard by the ships that sail the seas!"

"There are no ships in the sky," observed Cazévon.

"Oh, yes, there are," Barnett contradicted him, "only we don't think of them as that. We call them balloons, and aeroplanes, and—after all, air-ships! They ride the air as ships ride the ocean, and any number of things may fall or be thrown overboard from them! Suppose one of these things is a coil of rope, which slips over the battlements of the Old Dungeon, and there you have the solution of the mystery."

"A nice, convenient explanation!"

"Pardon me, an extremely well-founded explanation. If you glance through the local papers for the past week, as I did yesterday, you will see that a balloon flew over this part of the country on the night preceding Jean d'Alescar's death. It was travelling from north to south, and ballast was heaved overboard ten miles north of Guéret. The obvious inference is that a coil of rope was also thrown out, that one end got caught in a tree on the terrace, and to free it Jean d'Alescar had to break off a branch. He then went down to the terrace, tied the two ends of the rope together, and climbed up to the tower. Not an easy thing to do, but possible for a lad of his years."

"And then?" came in a whisper from Cazévon, whose face had grown suddenly gray.

"Then," Barnett continued, "someone who was standing here, at this window, and who was a remarkable shot, observed the boy hanging suspended in midair, took aim at the rope, and—severed it!"

Cazévon made a choking noise.

"That is your explanation of the—accident?"

Barnett took no notice of the interruption, but went on:

"Afterwards, this person hurried to the bank of the Creuse and searched the dead body to get the receipt. He took hold of the dangling rope, and hauled it down—then threw the highly compromising piece of evidence into a neighboring well—not a very safe hiding-place!"

The accusation had shifted to Georges Cazévon himself—a kind of guilty legacy from the man's dead father. The past was being linked up with the present—the net was closing in.

With a convulsive effort, Cazévon shook himself, as if to rid himself of Barnett's odious presence.

"I've had enough of your lies!" he shouted. "The whole thing's ridiculous invention on your part—you're simply making this up to terrorize me. I shall tell Monsieur Béchoux that I have had you thrown out as a common blackmailer. That's what you are, a blackmailer! But you won't get any change out of me!"

"If I had come here to blackmail you," said Barnett blithely, "I should have started off by producing my proofs."

Blind with rage, Cazévon screamed:

"Your proofs! What proofs have you got? Nothing but a cock-and-bull story. You haven't a single proof of any kind—how could you have? Why, there's only one proof that would be worth anything—only one. And if you can't produce that, then your whole story collapses at once, and you're a fool as well as a knave!"

"And what is that proof?" asked Barnett, still smiling.

"The receipt, of course! The receipt signed by my father!"

"Here it is," said Barnett, holding out a sheet of stamped paper, frayed and yellow at the edges. "This is your father's handwriting, isn't it? Pretty explicit, this document: '*I, the undersigned, Auguste Cazévon, hereby acknowledge the receipt from the Comte d'Alescar of the sum of two hundred thousand francs previously loaned to him by me, and I hereby declare that this repayment renders null and void any and every claim of mine to the Château and lands of Mazurech.*'

"The date," continued Barnett, "corresponds to that mentioned by Gréaume. The receipt is signed. Therefore it is indisputably genuine, and you, Cazévon, must have known about it from your father's own lips or from the private papers he left when he died. The discovery of this document meant disgrace for your father and yourself, and the loss of the Château, for which you felt all your father's attachment. That's why you killed d'Alescar!"

"If I had killed him," faltered Cazévon, "I should have removed the receipt from his body."

"You had a good look for it," said Barnett grimly, "but it wasn't on him. Jean d'Alescar had prudently wrapped it round a stone and thrown it down from the top of the tower, meaning to pick it up when he got to the ground again. I found it near the river, some twenty yards away."

Barnett only just stepped back in time to prevent Cazévon snatching the receipt from his hand. There was a moment's pause, and then Barnett, breathing a trifle quicker, spoke again:

"That is tantamount to admitting your guilt! Looking at you now, I can well believe Mademoiselle d'Alescar's statement that you are capable of almost anything. You are the slave of your own unreasoning impulse! Carried away by the passions of greed and hatred, you raised your gun and fired that morning. Steady, man!" as Cazévon seemed about to collapse, "control yourself. Someone's ringing! It must be Béchoux. Perhaps you won't want him to know all this!"

A full minute passed in silence. At last, Cazévon, his eyes still those of a maniac, whispered:

"How much? What must I pay you for the receipt?"

"It is not for sale."

"What do you mean to do with it?"

"It will be handed over to you, on certain conditions, which I will outline in Inspector Béchoux's presence."

"And if I refuse to accept your terms?"

"Then it will be my painful duty to expose you!"

"No one will believe you!"

"Oh, won't they?"

Cazévon's head slumped in utter dejection. Barnett's driving, implacable will-power had beaten him. At that moment Béchoux was shown in.

The inspector had not expected to find Barnett on the scene. He was unpleasantly surprised, and wondered what the two men could have been talking about; whether the incalculable Barnett had been busy digging pits for the luckless representative of the law to fall into.

Fearing something of the sort, he was quite aggressively positive in his assertions from the word "go."

Shaking Cazévon warmly by the hand he declared:

"Monsieur, I promised to let you know the result of my investigations before I left, and to tell you what kind of report I should make. So far, my own views are in complete accord with the construction that has been put upon the case. There is absolutely nothing in what Mademoiselle d'Alescar has been saying against you."

"Hear, hear," said Barnett. "That's just what I've been telling Monsieur Cazévon. Béchoux, my guide, philosopher and friend, is displaying his usual acumen. Nevertheless, the fact is that Monsieur Cazévon is bent on returning good for evil, and meeting calumny with generosity. He insists on restoring the domain of her ancestors to Mademoiselle d'Alescar!"

Béchoux looked thunderstruck.

"Wh—what? You mean to say——"

"Just that," said Barnett. "The affair has not unnaturally filled Monsieur Cazévon with distaste for the district, and he has his eye on a château nearer his factories in Guéret. When I got here this afternoon Monsieur Cazévon was actually drafting the deed of gift. He also expressed his wish to add a bearer check for one hundred thousand francs to be handed to Mademoiselle d'Alescar as compensation. That's so, isn't it, Monsieur Cazévon?"

Without a second's hesitation, Cazévon acted on Barnett's promptings as if they had been the dictates of his heart's desires. He seated himself at his desk, wrote out the deed of gift and signed the check.

"There you are," he said. "For the rest, I will instruct my solicitor."

Barnett took both check and document, slipped them into an envelope, and said to Béchoux:

"Here, take this to Mademoiselle d'Alescar. I feel sure she will appreciate Monsieur Cazévon's generosity. Monsieur, I am at your service. I cannot tell you how happy you have made us both by furnishing such a satisfactory solution to the business."

He swaggered off, followed by Béchoux. The latter, utterly astounded, waited till they were out of the park, and then demanded:

"What's it all mean? Did he fire that shot? Has he made a statement to you?"

"None of your business, Béchoux," said Barnett. "Let bygones be bygones. The case has been settled to everyone's best advantage. All you have to do is to speed on your mission to Mademoiselle d'Alescar. Ask her to forgive and forget, and not to breathe a word to anyone. Then come and pick me up at the inn."

In a short while Béchoux was back again. He brought the news that Mademoiselle d'Alescar had accepted the gift of the Mazurech estate and her solicitor would take the matter up at once, but the money she refused to take. In her indignation at being offered it she had torn up the check.

Barnett and Béchoux took their leave. The return journey was made in silence. The inspector was lost in unprofitable speculation. His mind was in a whirl of interrogation, but Barnett looked disinclined for confidential converse.

They got to Paris at close on to three o'clock. Barnett invited Béchoux to lunch with him near the Bourse, and Béchoux, incapable of resistance, went with him meekly.

"You do the ordering," said Barnett, rising from the table a moment after they had entered the restaurant. "I've some business I must attend to. Won't be a moment!"

Béchoux did not have long to wait. Barnett was back again almost immediately, and the two men ate a hearty meal. When they were drinking their coffee, Béchoux ventured a remark:

"I must send the torn bits of that check back to Monsieur Cazévon."

"Oh, I shouldn't bother to do that, Béchoux."

"Why not?"

"The check was quite worthless."

"But how?"

"Oh," said Barnett airily, "I foresaw that Mademoiselle d'Alescar was certain to refuse to take it, so when I put the deed of gift into the envelope I slipped in with it an old cancelled check. Waste not, want not."

"But what happened to the genuine check?" groaned Béchoux, "the one Monsieur Cazévon signed?"

"Oh, *that*! I've just been and cashed it at the bank!"

He opened his coat, displaying a wad of notes. Béchoux's coffee cup slipped from his nerveless grasp. With an effort he controlled himself.

For a long while they sat smoking in silence, facing one another across the table. At last Barnett spoke:

"There's no denying it, Béchoux, so far our collaboration has proved decidedly fruitful. We seem to ring the bell every time, and it's all helped to enlarge my little nest-egg. But, honestly, I'm beginning to feel very troubled about you, old horse. Here we are, working side by side, and I always pocket the dibs. Look here, Béchoux, won't you come into partnership with me? The Barnett and Béchoux Agency? It really sounds rather well!"

Béchoux gave him a look of hatred. The man goaded him beyond endurance. He rose, flung down a note to pay for the lunch, and mumbled as he took his leave:

"There are times when I think it must be Arsène Lupin after all!"

"I sometimes wonder, too," said Barnett—and laughed.

CHAPTER IX

DOUBLE ENTRY

A serious breach in the Béchoux-Barnett friendship seemed to have been caused by the affair of the Old Dungeon at Mazurech, and the fleecing of Georges Cazévon, so that when a taxi came to a halt in the *rue Laborde* and Inspector Béchoux leapt from it and hurled himself into the office of his friend, Jim Barnett, no one was more surprised than the latter.

"This is indeed a pleasure," he said, advancing with alacrity. "Our last parting was rather in silence and tears, and I was afraid you were feeling sore. And is there anything I can do for you in a small way this merry morning?"

"There is."

Barnett shook the inspector warmly by the hand.

"Splendid! But what's up? You look positively apoplectic. Please don't burst in *my* office."

"Kindly be serious, Barnett," said poor Béchoux stiffly. "I'm working on a most complicated case from which I particularly want to emerge triumphant."

"What's it all about?"

"My wife," said Béchoux, and there was anguish in his tone.

Barnett's eyebrows shot up.

"Your wife?" he echoed. "Then you're married?"

"Been divorced six years," was the laconic answer.

"Incompatibility?"

"No. My wife found she had a vocation for the stage! The stage—I ask you! Married to an inspector of police and she wanted to go on——" Béchoux sneezed abruptly and violently, giving Barnett time to ask:

"Then she became an actress?"

"A singer."

"At the Opéra?"

"No. The Folies Bergère. She's Olga Vaubant."

"What, not the lady who does the Acrobatic Arias? But she's wonderful, Béchoux. Olga Vaubant is a superb artiste. She has created a new art form.

Her latest number brings down the house. It's sheer genius—absolutely. You know, she stands on her head and sings:

> *" 'I'm in luck, I gotta boy*
> *Fills his momma's heart with joy—*
> *Yes, you otta see my Jim!'*
> *And she's your wife!"*

"Was," said Béchoux shortly. "Well, I'm glad you like the lady's performance. I've just been honored with a note from her."

He produced a sheet of rose-colored notepaper, with an embossed crimson O in one corner. Scrawled in pencil and dated that very morning was the following message:

> *"My bedroom suite has been stolen. Mother in a state of collapse.*
> *Come at once.—Olga."*

"The moment I got this," said Béchoux, "I telephoned the préfecture. They had already been called in on the case, and I obtained permission to collaborate with the men who are handling it."

"Then why are you all of a dither?" asked Barnett.

"It's—it's because this will mean meeting her again," said Béchoux, ashamed and furious.

"Are you still in love with her?"

"Whenever I see her—it's idiotic, but something comes over me—I can't help myself. I feel myself blushing like a schoolboy. My mouth goes dry and I begin stammering. You must see, Barnett, that I can't take charge of the case like that. I should make a perfect fool of myself."

"Whereas, what you *want* to do is to impress madame with the cool dignity, the daring and resource that go to make Inspector Béchoux the Pride of Paris Police?"

"Er—yes."

"And you look to me to help you. Béchoux, you can count on me. Now tell me, what sort of life does your ex-wife lead off the stage?"

Béchoux looked almost pained at the question.

"She is above suspicion and lives for her art alone. If it weren't for her profession, Olga would still be Madame Béchoux."

"Which would be a nation's loss," pronounced Barnett solemnly, gathering up hat and coat.

A few minutes later the two men came to one of the quietest, most deserted streets near the Luxembourg. Olga Vaubant lived on the top floor of an old-fashioned house whose bricks breathed respectability. The ground-floor windows were heavily barred.

"Before we go any further," said Béchoux, "I am going to suggest that in this instance you refrain from playing your own hand and making a dishonorable private profit out of the case, as you have unhappily been known to do in the past."

"My conscience ..." began Barnett, but Béchoux waved away the objection.

"Never mind *your* conscience," he said. "Think of the way mine has pricked me whenever we've worked together!"

"You don't think I'd rob your own ex-wife? Oh, Béchoux, how you wrong me!"

"I don't want you to rob *anyone*," said Béchoux.

"Not even those who deserve it?"

"Leave Justice to take its course. Heaven has not appointed you as an avenging angel."

Barnett sighed.

"You are spoiling all my fun, Béchoux, but what you say goes."

One policeman was on guard at the door, and another was with the concierges—husband and wife—who were badly upset by what had happened.

Béchoux learned that the district superintendent and two headquarters' men had just left after making a preliminary investigation.

"Now's our chance," said Béchoux to Barnett. "Let's get a move on while the coast is clear."

As they went up the staircase he explained to his friend that the house was run on old-fashioned lines, and the street door was kept shut.

"No one has a key, and everyone has to ring for admittance. A priest lives on the first floor and a magistrate on the second. The concierge acts as housekeeper to both of them. Olga has the top floor flat and leads a most conventional existence, complete with her mother and two old maidservants who have always been in the family."

They knocked at the door of Olga Vaubant's flat, and one of the maids let them into the hall. Béchoux rapidly explained the position of the rooms to Barnett—the passage on the right led to Olga's bedroom and boudoir, that on the left to her mother's room and the servants' quarters. Straight ahead was a studio fitted up as a gymnasium, with a horizontal bar, a trapeze, rings, ropes and ribstalls. Strewn about the place were Indian clubs, dumb-bells, foils, and so forth.

As the two men entered this vast room, something seemed to drop in a heap at their feet from the sky-light. The heap resolved itself into a slender, laughing boy, with a mop of untidy red hair framing the delicate features of a charming face. Wide green eyes, tip-tilted nose, slightly crooked mouth—all were unmistakable, and Barnett immediately recognized in the pajama-clad "boy" the one and only Olga Vaubant. She exclaimed at once in the Parisian drawl that has its parallel in the Londoner's cockney:

"*Maman's* all right, Béchoux. Sleeping like a top, bless her. Lucky, isn't it?"

She made a sudden dive floorwards, stood on her hands and, with her feet waving in the air, began singing in a husky, thrilling contralto:

> "*I'm in luck, I gotta boy,*
> *Fills his momma's heart with joy—*

And believe me, Béchoux, you fill my heart with joy, too, old dear," she added, standing up. "You're a real sport to have got here so soon. Who's the boy-friend?"

"Jim Barnett. He's an old—acquaintance," said Béchoux, vainly attempting to control his twitching countenance.

"Fine," said Olga. "Well let's hope between the pair of you you'll solve the mystery and get back my bedroom suite. I leave it to you. Now it's my turn to do a bit of introducing," as a bulky form hove up from the far end of the studio. "May I present Del Prego, my gym instructor? He's masseur, make-up expert, and beauty doctor, and he's the darling of the chorus. Regular osteopath, he is, for dislocation and rejuvenation! Say pretty to the gentlemen, Del Prego!"

Del Prego bowed low. He was a broad-shouldered, copper-skinned fellow, genial of countenance and vaguely suggesting the clown in his appearance. He wore a grey suit, with white spats and gloves, and held a light-colored felt hat in his hands.

Immediately, gesticulating violently and speaking with a marked foreign accent, he began to discourse on his method of "progressive dislocation," larding his outlandish French with phrases in Spanish, English, and Russian. Olga cut him short.

"We've no time to waste. What do you want me to tell you, Béchoux?"

"First," said Béchoux, "will you show us your bedroom?"

"Right! Half a mo'." She sprang up in the air, caught on to the trapeze, swung from that to the rings, and landed at a door in the wall on the right.

"Here you are," she told them, kicking it open.

The room was absolutely empty. Bed, chairs, curtains, mirrors, rugs, dressing-table, ornaments, pictures—all gone. Furniture removers could not have made a better job of it. The place was stripped.

Olga began to giggle helplessly.

"See that? Thorough, weren't they? They even pinched my ivory toilet set. Almost walked off with the floor-boards. Don't you think it's a shame, Mr. Barnett?" she went on, addressing Jim, her eyes wider than ever. "I'm a girl that's real fond of good furniture. All pure Louis Quinze it was, that I'd collected bit by bit—and they all had a history, including a genuine Pompadour bed! Why, furnishing this room cost me nearly everything I made on my American tour."

Abruptly she broke off to turn a somersault, then tossed the hair off her face and went on cheerfully:

"Oh, well, there's plenty of good fish in the sea and I can replace all that lot. I needn't worry so long as I have my india rubber muscles and my bee-yewtiful cracked voice.... What are you looking at me like that for, Béchoux? Going to faint at my feet? Give us a kiss, and let's get on with any questions you want to ask before we have the rest of the police force back on the scene."

"Tell me exactly what happened," said Béchoux.

"Oh, there isn't much to tell," answered Olga. "Let's see, last night, it had just gone half-past ten.... Oh, I should have told you, I left here at eight with Del Prego, who escorted me to the Folies Bergère in *maman's* place.... Well, as I was saying, it had just gone the half-hour, and *maman* was in her room knitting, when suddenly she heard a faint sound like someone moving about in my room. She rushed along the passage, and found two men taking my bed apart by the light of a flash-lamp! The light was switched off at once, and one chap sprang at her and knocked her down while the other flung a tablecloth over her head. How's that for assault and battery? Poor old *maman*! Then, if you please, these two blighters calmly proceeded to remove the furniture bit by bit, one of them carrying it downstairs, while the other stayed in the room. *Maman* kept quiet and managed not to scream. After a while she heard a big car starting up in the street outside, and then she was so overcome with the strain that she fainted right off."

"So that when you got back from the show——?" prompted Béchoux.

"I found the street door open, the flat door open, and *maman* lying unconscious on the floor of my room. You could have knocked me down with a feather!"

"What had the concierges to say?"

"You know them, Béchoux. Two old dears who've been here for thirty years now. An earthquake wouldn't rouse 'em. The only sound they ever hear is the door-bell. Well, they swear by all their gods that no one rang between ten o'clock, when they went to bed, and next morning."

"Which means," said Béchoux, "that they had no cause at any time during the night to pull the string that opens the door."

"You've said it."

"Did the other tenants hear nothing?"

"Nothing at all."

"Then the conclusion is——"

"How do you mean, conclusion?"

"Well, what do you make of it?"

Olga's expression was one of wrath.

"Don't be an idiot! It's not my business to make anything of it. That's your job, Béchoux. In a moment you'll have me thinking you as big a fool as those policemen we've had all over the flat."

"But," faltered Béchoux, "we're only beginning."

"Can't you get action with what I've told you, you boob? If that pal of yours there isn't any brighter than you, I can bid my Pompadour bed a fond farewell!"

The "pal" at this point stepped forward and asked:

"On what particular day would you like your bed back, madame?"

"What's that?" said Olga, staring at this stranger to whom, up to now, she had paid but slight attention.

Barnett became glibly detailed.

"I should like to know the day and hour on which you desire to regain possession of your Pompadour bed and of your furniture, etcetera."

"Is this your idea of a joke?"

"Let's fix the day," said the imperturbable Barnett.

"To-day is Tuesday. Will next Tuesday be satisfactory?"

Olga's eyes widened, and widened yet again. She could not make Barnett out a bit. Suddenly she began to rock with mirth.

"You *are* a one, I must say! Where did you pick it up, Béchoux? Out of the asylum? I must say your friend's got a nerve. In a week, he says, cool as you please. You might think the bed was in his pocket! You've got another thing coming if you fancy I'm going to waste my time with two mutts like you." With a hand on the chest of each, she pushed them vigorously into the hall. "Out you go, my lads, and you can stay out! And don't think I'm going to let *myself* be fooled by a couple of rotten jokers!"

The studio door slammed violently on the two "rotten jokers," and Béchoux groaned aloud.

"And we've only been in the flat ten minutes!"

Barnett was calmly examining the hall. He then talked to one of the old servants. After that, he went downstairs to the concierges' quarters and questioned the pair of them. He then hailed a passing taxi, giving the driver his address in the rue Laborde. Inspector Béchoux, deserted and aghast, stood forlornly on the pavement and watched the disappearing chariot of his friend.

However much Jim Barnett held Inspector Béchoux spellbound, the latter stood in even greater awe of the imperious Olga. He never dreamed of doubting her assertion that Barnett had turned the whole thing off by making a promise no one could take seriously.

This gloomy view of affairs was confirmed next day when he called at the office in the *rue Laborde* and found Barnett lolling back in an armchair, his feet upon his desk, smoking peacefully.

"Really, Barnett," said Béchoux in exasperation, "if this is your idea of getting down to things, we may as well give up the case. Back at the house we're all hopelessly at sea. We none of us know what to make of it. We are agreed on certain points, of course. The main thing is, that it's a physical impossibility to enter the place, even using a skeleton key, unless the door is opened from the inside. Since none of the residents can be suspected of being concerned in the burglary, we are driven to two unavoidable conclusions: first, that one of the thieves had been in the house, concealed, since early in the evening, and this man let in a confederate; second, that he could not have got inside without being seen by one of the concierges, as the street door is never left open. But who can have been in the house ready to admit the other thief? That's what floors us, and I don't see how on earth we're going to find it out. Have you any theory, Barnett?"

But Barnett was silent, absorbed in blowing smoke-rings. Béchoux's words might have fallen on deaf ears, but he continued:

"We've made a list of people who called during that day—there weren't many—and the concierges are positive that every single one of them left the house again. So you see we're without a clue. We can easily reconstruct the *modus operandi* of the crime, but its authors elude us. What do you make of it all?"

Barnett gave a prodigious yawn, stretched his arms and legs till they cracked, and then drawled:

"A perfect peach!"

"Wh-what's that? Who're you calling a peach?"

"Your ex-wife," Barnett told the astonished Béchoux. "She's as much of a knock-out off the stage as she is on. So full of *joie de vivre*, so—so electric! A regular *gamine*. Wonderful taste, too. I just can't get over the idea of her investing her earnings in that Pompadour bed! Béchoux, you're a lucky dog!"

"I lost my luck pretty quickly—only kept it a month!"

"A whole month? Then what *are* you grumbling at?"

Next Saturday saw Béchoux back at the Barnett Agency, trying to rouse his torpid ally, but Barnett was wreathed in smoke and silence, and Béchoux got no satisfaction.

On Monday he came in again, thoroughly depressed.

"It's a mug's game," he averred, "the men on the job are utter idiots, and all this time Olga's bedroom suite is probably on its way to some port or other for shipment abroad. It's maddening! And what do you suppose all

118

this makes me look like to Olga—me, a police inspector, I ask you? Why, she thinks I'm the most colossal ass that ever stepped."

He glared at the imperturbable Barnett, absorbed in his eternal smoke-rings, and let loose the full force of his fury.

"Here are we, up against an entirely new type of criminal—fighting men who must be adepts in their own line—and there you sit, you—you lotus-eater, and don't lift a finger to help!"

"One quality in her," said Barnett, musing aloud, "pleases me more than all."

"*What?*" shouted Béchoux.

"Her naturalness—her superb spontaneity. She is absolutely devoid of anything theatrical, any pose. Olga says exactly what she means, follows her instincts and lives according to impulse. Béchoux, she's a marvel!"

Béchoux brought his fist down on the desk with a bang.

"Would you like to know what she thinks of *you*? She thinks you're a D-U-D, dud! She and Del Prego can't mention your name without hooting. They speak of you as 'That boob Barnett—that crazy bluffer'...."

Barnett heaved a sigh.

"Harsh words! How can I prove the cap doesn't fit?"

"By ceasing to wear it," suggested Béchoux grimly. "To-morrow is Tuesday, and you've promised to produce that Pompadour bed!"

"Good lord, so I have!" said Barnett, as if realizing it for the first time. "The trouble is, I haven't the faintest idea where to look for it! Be a sports-man, Béchoux, and ladle out a word of advice."

"If you can lay hold of the thieves, they'll know where to find the bed."

"It might be done," said Barnett. "Got a warrant?"

Béchoux nodded.

"Right. Then telephone the *préfecture* to send two of their beefiest men today to the Odéon Arcades, near the Luxembourg."

Béchoux looked both surprised and irresolute.

"No fooling?"

"Absolutely not. Do you think I relish being thought a boob by Olga Vaubant? And, anyway, don't I always keep my promises?"

Béchoux thought hard for a moment. Something told him that Barnett meant what he said, and that during the last week, while he had lolled in his armchair, his brain had been alert and busy with the problem. He remem-bered Barnett's dictum that there were times when meditation proved more profitable than investigation. Without further hesitation, Béchoux took up the telephone and called up one, Albert, who was the right-hand man of the chief. He arranged for two inspectors to be sent to the Odéon.

Barnett heaved himself out of his chair, and the clock struck three as the two men left the Agency.

"Are we going to Olga's flat?" Béchoux asked.

"To that of the concierges," Barnett told him.

When they arrived Barnett conversed in low tones with the concierges and asked them to say nothing of his and Béchoux's presence in the house. They then stationed themselves in the rear of the concierges' quarters, concealed behind a voluminous bed-curtain. By peering out at each side, they could see anyone leave the house, or enter it when the door was opened.

They saw the priest from the first floor pass. Then came one of Olga's old servants, carrying a market-basket.

"Who on earth are we waiting for?" whispered Béchoux. "What's your game?"

"To teach you your job! Now then, not another word!"

At half-past three Del Prego was admitted, resplendent in white gloves, white spats, grey suit and grey Stetson. He waved a greeting to the concierges and went up the stairs two at time. It was the hour for Olga's gym lesson.

Three-quarters of an hour later he left the house, returning shortly with a packet of cigarettes he had gone out to buy. His white gloves and spats flickered up the stairs.

Three other people came and went. Suddenly Béchoux hissed in Barnett's ear:

"Look, he's coming in again for the third time. How on earth did he get out?"

"By the door, I suppose."

"Oh, surely not," said Béchoux, albeit less authoritatively. "That is, unless he caught us napping. Eh, Barnett?"

Barnett pushed back the curtain and answered:

"The time has come for action. Béchoux, go and pick up your beefy friends."

"And bring them here?"

"That's the stuff."

"What about you?"

"I'm going up aloft. When you get back, I want all three of you to station yourselves on the landing of the second floor. You'll get word when to move."

"Then it's zero at last?"

"It is, and pretty stiff odds. Now, off you go, and make it snappy."

Béchoux was off like the wind, while Barnett mounted to the third floor and rang the flat bell. He was shown into the studio-gymnasium where Olga was finishing her exercises under Del Prego's supervision.

"Fancy that now, here's that bright boy Barnett!" called Olga from the top of a rope-ladder. "Our Mr. Barnett, the Man of Mystery!" She peered at him from between her shapely legs. "Well, Mr. Barnett, I hope you've got my Pompadour bed with you!"

"Almost, but not quite, madame. I hope I'm not in the way?"

"Not a bit."

The incredible Olga continued her evolutions at Del Prego's curt commands. Her instructor alternately praised and criticised, and occasionally gave a brief personal demonstration. He was himself a trained acrobat, but vigorous rather than supple. He seemed out to demonstrate his prodigious muscular strength.

The lesson came to an end, and, Del Prego put on his coat, fastened his snowy spats, and gathered up his white gloves and ash-colored hat.

"See you tonight at the theatre, Madame Olga," he said.

"Oh, aren't you going to wait for me to-day, Del Prego? You might have escorted me. You know *maman* is away."

"Impossible, madame, I fear. Much as I regret, I fear I have another appointment before dinner."

He made for the door, but before he got there he was brought up short by Jim Barnett, who stood in his way.

"A word with you, my friend," said Barnett, "since chance has obligingly brought us together."

"I'm sorry, but really...."

"Must I, then, introduce myself afresh? Jim Barnett, private detective, of the Barnett Agency—Inspector Béchoux's friend."

Del Prego took another step towards the door.

"A thousand apologies, Mr. Barnett, but I'm in rather a hurry."

"Oh, I won't keep you a moment. I only want to call to your remembrance———" He paused dramatically.

"What?" snapped Del Prego.

"A certain Turk."

"I don't understand what you mean."

"A Turk called Ben-Vali."

The professor's face wore an expression of stony blankness.

"The name means nothing to me."

"Then perhaps you may remember a certain Avernoff?"

"Never heard of him either. Who were they both, anyway?"

"Two—murderers."

There was a brief, pregnant pause. Then Del Prego laughed noisily and said:

"Scarcely a class among which I care to cultivate my friendships."

"And yet," pursued Barnett, "rumor persists in urging that you knew both men well."

121

Del Prego's glance travelled like lightning up and down Barnett's form. Then he snarled, with scarcely a trace of foreign accent:

"What are you getting at? Cut out the mystery stuff. I don't go in for riddles."

"Sit down, Signor Del Prego," suggested Barnett. "We can chat more comfortably sitting down!"

Del Prego was fuming with impatience. Olga had come up to them, full of curiosity, looking like a bewitching boy in her gym kit.

"Do sit down, Del Prego," she said, laying a hand on the professor's arm. "After all, it's about my Pompadour bed."

"Just so," said Barnett. "And I can assure Signor Del Prego that I am not asking a riddle. Only, on my very first visit here after the robbery, I was forcibly reminded of two cases that made rather a sensation some time ago. I should like his opinion on them. It'll only take a few minutes."

Barnett's attitude had subtly changed from one of deference to one of authority. His tone was unmistakable in its note of command. Olga Vaubant found herself feeling impressed by this strange man. Del Prego, overborne, merely growled:

"Hurry up, then!"

Barnett began his story:

"Once upon a time—three years ago, to be precise—there lived in Paris a jeweller called Saurois. He and his father shared a big top-floor flat. This jeweller formed a business connection with a man named Ben-Vali. The latter went about in a turban and full Turkish costumes, baggy trousers and all, and traded in second-grade precious stones, such as oriental topazes, irregular pearls, amethysts, and so forth. Well, one evening, on a day when Ben-Vali had called several times at his flat, Saurois came back from the theatre and found his father stabbed to death, and all his jewels gone. The inquiry revealed that the crime had been committed not by Ben-Vali himself—he produced an unshakable alibi—but by someone he must have brought round in the afternoon. But they never managed to lay hands on the assassin, nor on the Turk. The case was shelved. Do you remember, now?"

"I've only been in Paris two years," Del Prego parried swiftly. "And, anyway, I don't see the point...."

Jim Barnett went on:

"Nearly a year before that a similar crime took place. The victim in this case was a collector of medals called Davoul. It was established that the man who killed him was brought to his place and hidden by a Count Avernoff, a Russian, who wore an astrakhan cap and a long overcoat."

"Why, I remember that," exclaimed Olga Vaubant, who had turned suddenly pale.

122

"I saw at once," continued Barnett, "that between these two cases and the burglary of your bedroom there existed not, perhaps, a very close analogy, but a certain family resemblance. The robberies of Saurois the jeweller and of Davoul the medal collector were both the work of a pair of foreigners, and here again the method is identical. I mean, in each case there was the introduction of an accomplice who was responsible for the actual crime. The problem is—how were those accomplices introduced? I own that at first this completely baffled me. For the last few days I have been thrashing the solution out in silence and solitude. Working with the two given quantities, so to speak, of the Ben-Vali crime and the Avernoff crime, I set myself to reconstruct the general scheme—the 'constant'—of a crime-system that had probably been applied in many other cases unknown to me."

"And did you succeed?" asked Olga breathlessly.

"I did," Barnett told her. "Frankly, the idea is superb. It's the highest form of art—a manifestation of creative genius, wholly original in conception and execution. While the ordinary run of thieves and gun-men work with great secrecy, disguising themselves sometimes as plumbers or commercial travellers to gain entrance to a house, these people keep full in the limelight, and do the job without any attempt at concealment. The more observation they meet with, the better pleased they are. The method is for one of them quite openly to enter a house where he is already a frequent visitor, and his comings and goings are familiar to the residents. Then, on a chosen day, he goes out … and comes in again … and goes out once more … and comes in yet again … and then, while this man is in the house, *another* man comes in who is so like the first man in appearance that no one spots the difference! And there you have your accomplice introduced. The first man leaves the house again, quite openly, and his accomplice remains there concealed. Then, in the watches of the night, the first man returns to the house, and is admitted by the accomplice. Ingenious, isn't it?"

Then, with a peculiar intensity in his tone, Barnett went on, now directly to Del Prego:

"It's genius, Del Prego, absolute genius. Ordinary crooks, as I said, try to make themselves as inconspicuous as possible in their criminal pursuits. They wear nondescript, neutral clothing, and do their best to merge with their surroundings like creatures of the jungle. But the men I'm telling you about realized that the great thing in their scheme was to make a vivid and outstanding impression—to attract plenty of attention. A Russian wearing a fur cap, or a Turk in baggy trousers is a conspicuous and unusual figure. If such a man is habitually seen four times a day going up and downstairs in a house, no one will notice whether he comes in once oftener than he goes out. The point is, though, that the fifth time he comes in, it's the accomplice! And no one suspects it. That's how it's done, and I take my hat off to the inventor. It stands to reason that a man must be a master criminal to evolve and apply such a method—the kind of arch-crook who only occurs once in a generation. To me it is obvious that Ben-Vali and Count Avernoff are the same person. From this, isn't it only logical to conclude that this man has materialized a third time, in yet another guise, in the particular case which concerns us? He began by being a Russian, later on he appeared as a Turk, and this time—well, who comes here who, besides being a foreigner, dresses rather unusually?"

There was a dead silence. Olga put out a hand towards Barnett as if to stop him from she hardly knew what. She had only just tumbled to what he had been leading up to all this time, and the realization frightened her.

"No, no!" she cried. "I won't have you accusing people!"

Del Prego smiled blandly.

"Come, come, Madame Olga, don't get upset. Mr. Barnett will have his little joke."

"That's it, Del Prego," said Barnett, "I *will* have my little joke. You're perfectly right not to take my yarn of mystery and adventure seriously—that is, not until you know the finish. Of course, there's the obvious fact that you're a foreigner, and that your get-up is calculated to attract attention. White gloves … white spats…. And, of course, too, you've got one of those mobile, india rubber faces, which could pretty easily turn you from a Russian into a Turk, and from a Turk into a shady adventurer, nationality unspecified! *And*, of course, you're well known in this house, and business brings you here several times a day. But, after all, your reputation for honesty is unblemished, and you enjoy the patronage of no less a person than Olga Vaubant. So no one would *dream* of accusing *you*.

"But what was I to think? You see my difficulty, don't you? You were the only possible suspect, and yet you were above suspicion. Isn't that so, madame?" He turned to Olga for confirmation.

"Oh, yes," she agreed, eyes feverishly bright. "Then who *are* we to suspect? How can we find out who did it?"

"Aha," said Barnett, "that's simple enough. I've set a trap for the mystery mouse!"

"A trap? How could you do that?"

"Tell me, madame," said Barnett, "Baron de Laureins telephoned you on Saturday? I thought so. And yesterday he came to see you here?"

Olga nodded, full of wonder.

"And he brought you a chest full of silver, engraved with the Pompadour crest?"

"That's it," said Olga, "on the table. But——"

Barnett cut her short. In the manner of a fortune-teller he continued:

124

"Baron de Laureins, who is very hard up, is trying to sell the silver which is a family heirloom that has come down to him from the d'Etoiles, and he has left it in your care until tomorrow."

"How ... how do you know all this?" Olga was quite scared.

"I," said Barnett, "and the Baron—very new *noblesse*! Have you displayed the handsome silverware to your admiring friends?"

"Certainly."

"And, on the other hand, I take it your mother has had a telegram from the country, summoning her to the bedside of your ailing aunt?"

"How on earth do you know *that*?"

"I sent the telegram. Oh, believe me, I'm the whole works! So your mother went off this morning, and the chest stays in this room till tomorrow. What a temptation for the unknown friend who so cleverly burgled your bedroom to get up to his tricks again and snaffle the chest of silver. Much easier than a suite of furniture!"

Olga, now thoroughly alarmed, demanded:

"Will the attempt be made tonight?"

"Of course it will," Barnett assured her.

"Oh, how awful!" she wailed.

Del Prego, who had listened to all this in silence, now got up.

"What's so awful, madame?" he asked, with a faint sneer. "Forewarned is forearmed. You have only to ring up the police. With your permission, I will do so at once."

"Oh, dear me, no," protested Barnett. "I shall need you, Del Prego."

"I fail to see in what way you can require my services."

"Why, in helping to arrest the accomplice, of course!"

"Plenty of time for that, if the attempt is to be made tonight."

"Yes, but *do* bear in mind," urged Barnett gently but firmly, "that the accomplice was, in each case, introduced beforehand!"

"You mean he's already in the flat?" asked Del Prego.

"He's been here for the last half-hour," declared Barnett.

"Since I arrived, you mean?"

"Since you arrived the second time," said Barnett quietly. "I saw him as plainly as I see you now."

"Then he's hiding in the flat?"

Barnett pointed to the door.

"In the hall there's a clothes cupboard which hasn't been opened all the afternoon. He's in there."

"But he couldn't have got into the flat on his own!"

"Of course not."

"Then who opened the door to him?"

"You, Del Prego."

The brief statement was almost shockingly abrupt.

Even though from the beginning of the conversation Barnett's remarks had been obviously aimed at the gym instructor, becoming increasingly plain in their import, yet this downright attack took Del Prego by surprise. Rage, fear, and the determination to act swiftly were easily discernible in his changed expression. Divining his adversary's perplexity, Barnett took advantage of it to run out into the hall. He jerked a man out of the cupboard, and pushed him, struggling, before him into the studio.

"Oh," cried Olga, utterly taken aback, "then it's true!"

The man was the same height as Del Prego. Like Del Prego he wore a grey suit and white spats. He had much the same type of greasy, mobile countenance.

"Milord has forgotten his hat and gloves," said Barnett, and clapped an ash-colored hat on the man's head, at the same time handing him a pair of white gloves.

Struck dumb with amazement, Olga drew slowly from the scene of action, and, never shifting her gaze from the two men, proceeded to climb a rope-ladder backwards. It had now fully dawned on her what kind of man Del Prego was, and what frightful risks she had run during the time spent in his company.

"Funny, isn't it?" Barnett said, laughing. "Not as like as twins, of course, but they're the same height and have much the same sort of physiog., and what with that and their dressing in duplicate, they might be brothers!"

The two crooks were recovering from their confusion, and simultaneously began to realize that, after all, they were only up against one man, and that a poor-looking specimen, with apparently a wretched physique under his shabby frock-coat.

Del Prego spluttered some words in a foreign language which Barnett translated immediately.

"No use speaking Russian," he observed, "to ask your friend if he's got a gun handy!"

Del Prego shook with rage and spoke again in a different language.

"Unluckily for you," Barnett told him, "I know Turkish inside out. Berlitz has nothing on me. Also, I think it only fair to tell you that Béchoux —you know, Olga's policeman husband that was—is waiting on the stairs with two friends. If that gun goes off, they will break down the door!"

Del Prego and the other man exchanged glances. They saw they were cornered, but they were the sort that doesn't give in without putting up a stiff fight.

Without seeming to move, they drew imperceptibly closer to Barnett.

"Fine!" the latter told them genially. "You propose to set upon me and finish me off at close quarters, do you? And when I'm done for, you'll try to elude Béchoux. Now then, madame, keep your eyes open and you'll see something! Tom Thumb and the two Giants! David and the twin Goliaths! Get a move on, Del Prego. Brace up, now! Try springing at my throat for a start!"

The distance between them had lessened again. The two men stood tense, ready to hurl themselves on Barnett.

But Barnett most unexpectedly forestalled them. In a flash he had dived to the floor, seized a leg of each and brought them crashing! Before they had time to counter, the head of each was being ground into the floor by an implacable, murderous hand. They gasped convulsively, choking in Barnett's vise-like grip. Their countenances took on a purple tinge.

"Olga!" called Barnett with perfect calm, "be a good girl and open the door and call Béchoux, will you?"

Olga dropped, monkey-like, from her ladder, and tottered rather than ran out of the room, calling "Béchoux! Béchoux!"

A moment later she returned with the inspector, babbling excitedly to him:

"*He* did it! Bowled them both over single-handed! I'd never have believed it of him!"

"Behold," said Barnett to Béchoux, "your two bright lads. Just slip the bracelets on them so that I can let 'em come up for breath! You needn't worry about fixing them too tightly. They'll come quietly, won't you, Del Prego? All lamb-like and pretty!"

He rose from the floor, gallantly kissed Olga's hand, while she regarded him in ever-growing wonder, and chortled gaily:

"How's that for a haul, Béchoux? Two of the most cunning criminals in Paris snared at last. Really, Del Prego, you must allow me to congratulate you on your methods!"

He dug the professor playfully in the ribs, while the latter was powerless, handcuffed to Béchoux, and continued jubilantly:

"My good man, you're a genius. Why, when Béchoux and I were on the watch downstairs, I, having tumbled to your trick, naturally saw that it was *not* you the third time, but Béchoux, who didn't know, soon swallowed the bait and really thought the gentleman in white gloves, white spats, grey hat and grey suit was the same Del Prego that he had already seen pass several times. So Del Prego the Second was able to go quietly upstairs, sneak through the door—which you had left ajar for him—and hide in the hall cupboard. Exactly the same tactics as you employed on the night when the bedroom suite disappeared into space. You can't deny it, Del Prego, you're a genius!"

Barnett was by now bubbling over with sheer exuberance. With a flying leap, he was astride the trapeze; in a moment he was twirling like a top round and round an upright pole; he swung on to a rope, then to the rings, then up the ladder he went, swaying like a sailor in the rigging. The tails of his ancient frock-coat flapped stiffly, disapprovingly behind him, the venerable garment seeming to protest against these unseemly gambols.

Olga gave a little gasp as he unexpectedly landed at her feet, bowing low.

"Feel my heart, madame; beating quite normally. And I'm not the least bit out of breath. Don't you wonder, Béchoux, how I keep in training?"

He snatched up the telephone and called a number.

"That the *préfecture*?... Extension two, please.... That you, Albert? Béchoux speaking.... It doesn't sound like my voice?... Well, I can't help that. Now then, listen. You can report that I have just arrested two murderers who are wanted for the Olga Vaubant robbery."

He hung up, and held out a hand to Béchoux.

"The laurels are all yours, old chap. Madame, it's time I took my leave. What's up, Del Prego? You are not regarding me with that warm affection I could desire!"

Del Prego was muttering furiously:

"There's only one man alive who could get the better of me ... only one...."

"Who's that?"

"Arsène Lupin!"

Barnett laughed as though he would split.

"Bully for you, my boy. You ought to have been a Professor of Psychology. And then you would never have got yourself into this mix-up!"

He had another joyous spasm, bowed to Olga, and went off in a gale of merriment, humming that catchy little tune:

"Yes, you otta see my Jim!"

* * * *

Next day, Del Prego, overwhelmed by the case against him, revealed the whereabouts of the garage in the suburbs in which he had hidden Olga Vaubant's bedroom suite. This was on the Tuesday. Barnett had fulfilled his promise.

Béchoux was sent out of Paris on a fresh case, and was away some days. When he got back he found a note from Barnett.

"You must own that I have played strictly fair. There hasn't been a sou of profit for me in the whole business—none of the 'pickings' that have distressed your gentle soul in the past. It is satisfaction for me to know that I retain your friendship and respect!"

That afternoon Béchoux, who had made up his mind to part brass-rags once and for all with Barnett, went along to the office in the *rue Laborde*.

The office was closed, and there was a notice on the door which read:

> "*Closed on account of a sudden attachment.*
> *Reopening after the honeymoon trip.*"

"And what the hell may that mean?" muttered Béchoux, smitten with sudden vague anxiety. He rushed off to Olga's flat. It was shut up. He rushed on to the Folies Bergère. There he was told that the star had paid a large forfeit to break her contract and had gone off on holiday.

"*Nom d'un Nom d'un Nom!*" spluttered Béchoux when he got out in the street. "Is it possible?… Instead of collaring some cash, can he have used his triumph to … can he have dared to…."

The cloud of suspicion grew bigger and blacker. Béchoux became frantic. How was he to learn the truth? Or rather, what course could he take that would keep the truth from him, and save him from appalling certainty in place of his suspicion?

But Barnett was not the man to leave his victim in peace. At intervals the unlucky Béchoux was the recipient of highly colored post-cards, scrawled with even more lurid legends:

"*Oh, Béchoux! One moonlight night in Rome!*"

"*Béchoux, next time you're in love, bring her to Sicily!*"

And from Venice: "*If you were here, Béchoux, I should have to stop you jumping in a canal!*"

"I will never forgive him this, never! He has outraged me past hope of pardon! Next time I will have my revenge!"

And, like a mocking echo, he seemed to hear Olga's husky tones:

> "*I'm in luck, I gotta boy*
> *Fills his momma's heart with joy.*
> *Yes, you otta see my Jim!*"

CHAPTER X

ARRESTING ARSÈNE LUPIN!

Suddenly, unexpectedly, the fight between Barnett and Béchoux, which had dragged on so long under cover, had reached the last round—in the open!

Inspector Béchoux sped through the arched gateway of the *préfecture* and across a couple of courtyards, took the stairs two at a time, and dashed, without pausing to knock, into the sanctum of his chief. Pale and breathless, he stammered:

"Arsène Lupin is mixed up in the Desroques case!"

The chief gave a startled exclamation.

"Surely not!"

"I saw him myself only a little while ago, outside Desroques' flat, and recognized him at once."

"Don't try and be funny, Béchoux. Nobody ever *recognizes* Arsène Lupin."

"*I* do!" declared Béchoux. "This time he's disguised as a private detective and calls himself Jim Barnett—you remember, the chap I told you about before, who left Paris a little while ago."

The chief gave a slight chuckle.

"Left with Olga Vaubant of the Folies Bergère, didn't he?"

"Yes," assented Béchoux wrathfully. "Olga Vaubant, the singing acrobat, and my ex-wife!"

"Well," said the chief, "what did you do when you—recognized Lupin?"

"I shadowed him."

"Without his knowing it?" The other was frankly incredulous.

Béchoux drew himself up stiffly. "When I shadow a man, chief, he never knows it," he declared. "All the same," he added thoughtfully, "although the beggar was pretending to be out for a stroll, he didn't take any chances. First he walked round the Place de l'Etoile. Then he went along the Avenue Kléber and stopped on the east side of the Rond Point du Trocadéro. Sitting on a bench there was a gipsy girl. She was a pretty piece of goods, with her black head bare in the sunshine, and her colored shawl wrapped about her. Well I watched Lupin, alias Barnett, sit down beside her, and a minute later they were talking away together, but hardly moving their lips—an old prison trick that, chief. More than once I noticed them looking up at a house on the corner of the Place du Trocadéro and the Avenue Kléber. After a while, Lupin got up and took the Metro."

"Did you keep on shadowing him?"

"Yes—or, rather, I tried to," said Béchoux. "But he jumped aboard a train that was just moving while I was held up in the crowd. When I got back to the bench, the gipsy girl was gone."

"And what about the house they were looking up at?"

"That's where I've just come from," said Béchoux. He took a deep breath, and launched forth: "On the fourth floor of that house is a furnished flat where for the last month old General Desroques, Jean Desroques' father, has been living. You remember that he came up from Limoges to defend his son when the latter was arrested and charged"—Béchoux swelled with the majesty of the law—"with abduction, illegal detention, and wilful murder!"

This repetition of the roll of crimes seemingly impressed the chief, who nodded solemnly and asked his subordinate:

"Did you call on the general?"

"I did, and he opened the door to me himself. Then I described to him the little comedy that had just been played under his windows, leaving out all mention of Arsène Lupin, of course. He was not surprised, and told me that the day before a gipsy girl had come to see him. She offered to tell his fortune and reveal the outcome of the trial. She demanded three thousand francs and said she would await his answer next afternoon in the Place du Trocadéro between two and half-past two."

"But why should the general pay her all that money?"

"She assured him that she could get hold of the mystery photograph and let him have it."

"What?" the chief was genuinely surprised. "You mean that photograph we've all been searching for and can't find anywhere?"

"That's it," said Béchoux. "The photograph that would save the general's son—or finally establish his guilt!"

Both were silent for a while. At last the chief said:

"I expect you know, Béchoux, how anxious we are to get hold of that photograph ourselves?"

Béchoux nodded.

"It means even more than you realize, though. Listen, Béchoux, if you can lay hands on that photograph it must be turned over to me before the Parquet gets wind of it." He added in a whisper: "The Department comes first, see?..."

And, with equal seriousness and set purpose, Béchoux replied, "Chief, you shall have it. I will get it for you, and, at the same time, I will get Jim Barnett, or rather Arsène Lupin!"

Just a month before this conversation at the *préfecture*, Jacques Veraldy had been kept waiting for his dinner. Jacques Veraldy, one of the foremost figures in Parisian society, a man of vast wealth, one of the unscrupulous spiders that spin political webs, had waited till long past the dinner hour for the return of his wife, Christiane. But she did not come home that night, and next morning the police were called in. They soon elicited the following facts:

On the afternoon of her disappearance, Christiane Veraldy had gone for a walk in the Bois de Boulogne, near her house. On this walk she had been stopped by a well-dressed man who, after a brief conversation, had led her to a closed car, with the blinds pulled down, which was waiting in a deserted alley. They both got into the car and drove off quickly in the direction of Saint-Cloud.

None of the witnesses who came forward to describe this meeting in the Bois had been able to see the man's face. He seemed young, they said, and they were all agreed that he wore a very smart dark-blue overcoat and a black beret.

Two days passed, and still there was no news of the missing Christiane Veraldy. Then, suddenly, the tragedy happened.

About sunset, some peasants working in the fields on the main road from Paris to Chartres noticed a car being driven at a reckless speed. Even as they watched its onrush, the car door was pushed open, and a woman fell out on the road. They rushed to her assistance. At the same time the car raced up the steep bank at the side of the road, crashed into a tree and overturned. A man sprang from it, miraculously uninjured, and dashed to where the woman lay. She was dead. Her head had struck a heap of stones in her fall. They carried her body to the nearest village and told the gendarmes what had happened.

The man made no secret of his identity. He was Député Jean Desroques, a well-known political figure, and at that time leader of the Opposition.

The dead woman was Christiane Veraldy.

Immediately trouble began brewing. The bereaved husband, thirsting for revenge rather than overcome with grief, was determined to make his supplanter, as he considered Jean Desroques, pay the penalty of the law. The accused man, on the other hand, had powerful political supporters, who strenuously denied that the leader of their party could be guilty of such a crime. These in turn brought pressure to bear on the police.

Meanwhile, the peasants, one and all, swore that they had seen a man's arm push the woman out of the car. Nor did there seem any possible doubt that the man who had been observed talking with Madame Veraldy in the Bois was indeed Desroques. At the time of the accident Jean Desroques was wearing a dark-blue greatcoat and a black beret.

In any case, Desroques did not attempt to advance an alibi. He admitted having abducted Madame Veraldy, and acknowledged that he had detained her illegally. On the other hand, he swore that he had done all in his power to prevent her committing—suicide! For that was his explanation of the tragic occurrence.

Desroques' account of what had happened was that he had been struggling to hold Madame Veraldy down in her seat, that the door of the car had been forced open when she flung her weight against it, and she had fallen out.

But concerning what had led up to the struggle, where they had spent the days since their meeting in the Bois, what had happened during that time, or even when and how he had first made the acquaintance of Madame Veraldy, Jean Desroques was obstinately silent.

This last point—the question of the first meeting of Desroques and the banker's wife—remained one of the minor yet most baffling mysteries of the case, since Veraldy declared he had never, since his marriage, had anything to do with Desroques, whom he regarded as a dangerous Radical. He testified to having frequently spoken disparagingly about him to Christiane, who had invariably refrained from comment.

The examining magistrate tried in vain to get past the accused's enigmatic barrier of reserve. The only reply his efforts elicited was:

"I have nothing to say. You can do what you like with me. Whatever happens I shall not speak another word."

And when the police officials, one of whom was Béchoux, called at Desroques' flat, he opened the door to them in person, saying:

"I am quite ready to come with you, gentlemen."

Before leaving, a thorough search was made of the flat. There was a pile of ashes in the study fireplace, showing that Desroques had been burning papers. The police found nothing of any importance in the drawers of the desk or anywhere else. They took down every volume from the well-stocked bookshelves and shook them vigorously, but no telltale document fluttered out to reward their efforts. They took up the carpet and discovered nothing but dust!

While this routine search was going on, Béchoux, pursuing his own rather more intuitive methods, stood perfectly still near the door and darted a lightning glance over the room. Suddenly he swooped down on the wastepaper basket. To one side of it lay a screw of paper which might have been an advertisement leaflet.

Béchoux had it in his hands and was just smoothing it out, when Jean Desroques, who had been standing quietly by during the search of his study, sprang forward and snatched it from the detective's hands.

"You don't want that," he cried, "its only an old photograph. It came off its mount and I threw it away."

Béchoux, struck by Desroques' eagerness to retain possession of an apparently worthless bit of rubbish that he had self-avowedly thrown away, was on the point of using force to make him give it up.

But Desroques was too quick for him. Before the detective could bar the way, he had darted into the adjoining room and slammed the door behind him.

There was a policeman on guard in the anteroom into which he had fled. When Béchoux and the others got the door open, this man had Desroques pinned on the floor. Immediately Béchoux searched his prisoner. He turned out the man's pockets, made him take off his shoes and socks. But the unmounted photograph had disappeared!

The window was tightly shut and there was no fire in the room. The policeman stated that he had stopped Desroques when he rushed in in case he should be trying to escape, but had seen no sign of any photograph or paper.

Béchoux had a warrant for Desroques' arrest, and, without vouchsafing a word, he went quietly off to prison.

The foregoing are the bare facts of the case which, a little while before the Great War, caused such a stir in the press and among the public of Paris. There is no need to give in detail the inquiry conducted by the examining magistrate, as it shed no light on the mystery. But there should be considerable interest in the relation for the first time of an episode which led up to certain startling disclosures and put an entirely different complexion on the case, besides marking the last encounter in the long duel between Inspector Béchoux and his "friendly enemy," Jim Barnett, of the Barnett Agency.

The stage was set, and for once Béchoux felt happy in the possession of a little advance information as to the program. He knew what Barnett was up to—had watched his little confabulation with the gipsy girl under the windows of General Desroques' flat. This time he intended to be first on the scene and to spoil Barnett's entrance!

On the day after the conversation with his chief at the *préfecture*, Béchoux again called at General Desroques' flat. The latter had been advised by headquarters of the inspector's visit.

A rather corpulent, clean-shaven man-servant opened the door to Béchoux. In silence, and exuding a kind of aura of intense respectability, he ushered the inspector into the drawing-room, then softly withdrew.

Béchoux took up his stand at a window from which he could survey the entire extent of the Place du Trocadéro without himself being seen from the street. For a long while he scrutinized the people passing to and fro in the busy square below.

There was no sign of the gipsy girl, nor of the wily "Barnett" in whom Béchoux declared he had recognized Arsène Lupin.

Neither of the suspects showed up all that day, nor the day after.

During his self-imposed vigil, Béchoux sometimes had the company of General Desroques. The latter was tall, lean, grey-haired—the typical retired cavalry officer who has spent much of his life outdoors, and is in the habit of giving orders and having them promptly obeyed. Ordinarily taciturn, the general was one of those men who, when deeply moved, will lay aside some of their customary reserve. The charge against his son had wounded him terribly. Not only was he firmly convinced of Jean's innocence, but he was certain that the young man was the victim of one of those mysterious political plots which occasionally blot the fair fame of every state.

Although undetermined as to whence the blow had come, the old man stood at bay—like a lion defending its cub.

"Jean would not, could not, do such a thing," he declared. "The boy's only fault is that he is over-scrupulous, absurdly quixotic. He is perfectly capable of sacrificing his own interests to some exaggerated idea of honor. He is the sort of person who would unhesitatingly shoulder a friend's guilt and let the culprit go free. I am so sure of what I say, that I'm not going to see Jean in his cell. I won't pay the slightest attention to what his lawyer says, or to what they print in the newspapers. Pack of lies, probably! The boy's innocent, whether he says so or not. And I'm going to prove it, whether he likes it or not! We all have our own idea of what's our duty. He thinks he ought to keep his mouth shut. Well and good. But I know *I* ought to clear his name, no matter who gets hurt in the process!"

One day, when the reporters were harrying him with questions, the general burst out:

"Do you really want to know what I think? Jean never kidnaped any one. The woman followed him of her own free will. He won't admit it, because he is trying to shield her reputation. But if the facts come to light—and, believe me, they will—we shall find that my son and she knew each other and were probably on terms of intimacy. And I'm going to get to the bottom of things, whatever the result!"

Now, while Béchoux crouched, like Sister Anne, at his window, and kept watch on the square, the general would come in and sit near him. Then the old man would go over the case and review the deadlock reached by himself and the police.

"You and I, my friend, are after the same thing," he would say, "but someone else is after it, too! I have friends who are in the know, and they tell me Veraldy has offered a fabulous reward to anyone who will solve the mystery of his wife's death. He and my son's political opponents are convinced that Jean is guilty. What we all want to find, though for very different reasons, is that photograph! Veraldy and his friends believe that if they can lay hands on it they will have proof of Jean's guilt. I *know* that it will prove him innocent!"

From Béchoux's point of view, what the photograph might or might not prove was the least of his worries. His task was limited to getting hold of it for his chief. Any possible sequel had almost ceased to interest him.

Meanwhile, day after day, he sat at his window watching for the gipsy girl who never came, filled with anguished speculation as to Barnett's activities, and listening inattentively to the general's eternal monologue about his hopes and plans and disappointments.

One day old Desroques seemed unusually thoughtful. He obviously imagined he had hit on a fresh clue, or, at any rate, a new factor in the tragic problem. After a prolonged silence he addressed Béchoux at his post:

"Inspector, my friends and I have come to the conclusion that the only human being who can possibly throw any light on how the photograph disappeared is the policeman who stopped my son in his flight the day he was arrested. It's rather curious that he has never been called to give evidence. His name has never appeared in the press. In fact, but for the energetic inquiries of my friends, I should not now be in possession of"—he paused significantly—"certain information!"

Inspector Béchoux looked distinctly uncomfortable, but did not speak. The general resumed:

"We now know that this policeman was added to the group of men sent here from headquarters quite accidentally, just as they were leaving the police-station of this district on their way here. They rather doubted whether their numbers were strong enough in case my son offered violent resistance, and this policeman apparently offered to join them with some alacrity. They gladly accepted his assistance.

"My friends have not been able to ascertain the identity of that policeman. For some reason or other none of your colleagues has been willing or able to tell us. Yet we are certain that the higher officials at the *préfecture* know who he is, and have been questioning him daily. We have reason to believe that he has been under strict surveillance ever since the arrest of my son. That he was taken to the police-station immediately after the disappearance of the photograph and searched; that he has not been allowed home; that he is, in fact, a prisoner. And we have more than an inkling of the reason for the strict reticence of the police on his account!" The general bent nearer to Béchoux, a certain triumph overspreading his hawklike features.

Outwardly calm and indifferent, Béchoux was quaking inwardly. But he said nothing, feeling it wisest to let the general put all his cards on the table.

"What do you say," said the general, "to the suggestion that the mysterious policeman was, to say the least of it, rather a peculiar character to have got into the police force at all? A nice story it would make for the newspapers—and not particularly creditable. Ho, ho!" He waggled a gouty finger under the inspector's nose.

Still Béchoux was silent.

"Well," said the general, "it isn't going to further my son's interests to make a laughing-stock of the police force. But what I do demand as a right is that I may be allowed to question this policeman myself. Your people haven't been able to get anything out of him. I think I may be more successful."

"And if I say that you cannot have this interview?" Béchoux's voice was cold and level as chilled steel.

"In that case, inspector, I shall—regretfully, of course—communicate with the editor of a well-known daily in regard to this somewhat curious ornament of the police force!"

"No need for that, general." Béchoux forced a smile. "There is no objection at all to your interviewing Constable Rimbourg—er, the policeman in question. I shall have pleasure in arranging for him to come along!"

In truth, Béchoux was not particularly unwilling in the matter. His own plans had proved fruitless. He was absolutely without information about Barnett's movements, and quite in the dark as to his adversary's connection with the case. In the past, Barnett had always met him openly, albeit under the guise of lending his aid. Barnett had even been noticeably to the fore throughout the cases on which he had "coöperated" with the inspector. Béchoux had an uneasy feeling that this time, for some reason of his own, Barnett was working under cover, ready to burst out at any moment with a startling and probably unwelcome *dénouement* of the whole affair. And then it would be too late to circumvent him!

His superiors gave Béchoux *carte blanche* to go ahead. Two days later, Sylvestre, the general's rotund man-servant, gravely ushered Béchoux and Constable Rimbourg into the drawing-room.

The constable was a very ordinary looking man—not at all the sort of figure to suggest a mystery. His eyes and mouth betrayed his weariness. He had been put through something of a "third degree" over the missing photograph. He was in uniform, with the customary revolver in a black leather case, and the policeman's baton—that world-wide symbol of law and order.

The general came in, and the three men sat a long while in conference. But no fresh light was shed on the problem of the photograph. Rimbourg was respectful, stolidly sympathetic, ready with his answers. But he denied having seen anything of any photograph.

Then the general changed the trend of his interrogations. Abruptly he asked:

"When did you first meet my son?"

"We did our military service together, sir," was the surprising answer.

"You said nothing of this," cried Béchoux.

"I was not asked about it, inspector," replied the man.

"I must tell you, general," said Béchoux, "that one of the reasons for our very strict surveillance of Constable Rimbourg was that he obtained his appointment through your son's influence!"

"What?" cried the general "But it has been freely hinted that this man, Rimbourg——" He broke off, suddenly thoughtful. Then he asked the constable: "What was your profession before you joined the police force?"

"I did various odd jobs, sir. I was carpenter and scene-shifter for a touring company. I travelled round with a circus. I was lift-man in a hotel."

"Why did you leave the hotel?"

"I tired of the job, sir." Rimbourg's voice was infinitely respectful, but there was a slight flicker in his eyes that belied his stolid calm.

"And you found the police force suited you?"

"Oh, perfectly, sir."

The general gave a disheartened shrug of dismissal.

"Thank you, thank you; that will do for the present, I think," he said. "I wish I could believe what you tell me, but frankly, I cannot help feeling you are keeping something back. Your previous acquaintance with my son is certainly an extraordinary coincidence, and I think, Inspector Béchoux, if I were you, I would investigate Constable Rimbourg's past a bit more closely. Find out why he left that job as lift-man. And remember what I said before about the suggestion that he is, perhaps, a curious kind of constable altogether. Look up some of the cases in which he has been concerned—it might prove illuminating!" He rang the bell. "Sylvestre, give Monsieur Rimbourg a drink before he goes." The door closed. "He'll be quite safe with my man," the general told Béchoux, as he poured out a glass of wine for the inspector. Then, raising his own glass:

"Here's to my son's speedy liberation," he said.

For a second Béchoux could have sworn he saw a gleam of triumphant merriment in the general's eye. A most uncalled-for emotion, surely, and yet....

He wheeled sharply round, for the general was grinning broadly now. The drawing-room door had swung silently open. On the threshold he beheld a strange manifestation. There was slowly approaching a creature that walked *on its hands*! The empurpled face almost touched the floor. Above it protruded a comfortable paunch, surmounted by a pair of oddly slim and wildly kicking legs that pointed ceiling-wards. For a moment Béchoux was forcibly reminded of the antics of his acrobat wife, Olga.

All at once the creature somersaulted, bringing its feet neatly together, and, right side up, began spinning round and round at terrific speed like a human top. And now Béchoux recognized—Sylvestre, the man-servant. Obviously the fellow was out of his mind. As he spun around, his stomach quivered like a jelly, and from his wide mouth issued a series of rousing guffaws.

But—was it really Sylvestre? As he watched the extraordinary performance, Béchoux felt his brow bathed in a clammy dew. *Could* this wild figure be the imperturbable, perfectly trained, intensely respectable man-servant?

The top ceased spinning. Sylvestre, if he it was, fixed the detective with a steady stare, relaxed his set expression of grotesque mirth, undid jacket and waistcoat, divested himself of *a rubber paunch*, and slipped gracefully into the coat which General Desroques handed him. Once more looking fixedly at the inspector he murmured solemnly:

"Sold again, Béchoux!"

And Béchoux, incapable of protest, sank weakly into a chair, breathing the one word—"Barnett...."

"Yes, Barnett," said the erstwhile man-servant, smiling.

And Barnett it was, but a resplendent Barnett. Gone was the air of shabby gentility, the seedy get-up. This new Barnett approximated more nearly to Inspector Béchoux's mental portrait of the redoubtable Arsène Lupin!

And the general was chuckling unrestrainedly!

Turning to him, Barnett bowed courteously.

"Forgive my antics, sir, but whenever something happens that especially delights me I am apt to cut a few capers out of sheer exuberance. I am sure you will understand."

"In this instance, my friend, you are surely entitled to behave like a whole circus of clowns. Your little plan has succeeded to perfection."

"What's all this?" asked Béchoux, recovering slightly from his first sense of shock and dismay. "Have you any special cause for joy, Barnett?"

"Why, yes, Béchoux; and the best of it is that it is all thanks to you, dear old chap. (He's the best of good fellows, general, I may tell you.) But I can see you are bursting to hear all about it. I will reserve my praises for another time, and start in on my little story."

He lit a cigarette, handing his case to the general, who also elected to smoke. Then, puffing appreciatively, he began:

139

"Well, Béchoux, a short while ago I was travelling in Spain with a lady, if you remember? Ah, I see you do. A friend of mine telegraphed, asking me to help in unravelling the Desroques case. As it happened, my little idyll was by then distinctly on the wane—a total eclipse of the honeymoon, if I may use the expression. I seized the chance of regaining my freedom. And fortune smiled on me. New lamps for old, Béchoux!

"For, at Granada, I fell in with a gipsy girl—a wild, southern beauty, Béchoux—and we travelled up together.

"I was attracted to the Desroques case chiefly, I own, because you were working on it. The more I thought about it, the more convinced I became that if there existed any proof of the guilt or innocence of Jean Desroques, it must be in the hands of the policeman who stopped him in his flight when they were making the arrest. But when I came to make investigations, I found myself up against a blank wall. I was unable to ascertain the identity of this man. I only guessed that he was being kept virtually a prisoner. What was I to do? Time was passing. The general and his son were both suffering severely under the strain. There was only one person in Paris who could help me—yourself!"

Béchoux did not move. He longed for the ground to open and swallow him up with his shame. He had been tricked once again, more thoroughly than ever before. Barnett had shown him up as being the typical, slow-witted detective, the butt of every mystery novelist!

"You were the only person who could help me," Barnett repeated, "for the reason that you, and only you, were in possession of the truth. You had been given the job of putting Rimbourg through the 'third degree.' But how was I to get in touch with you without your suspecting anything? How was I to work it so that you trotted off to retrieve the bird my chance shot had brought down?

"In the end I found an easy way. I deliberately let you shadow me. I led you along, like Follow-my-Leader, to the Place du Trocadéro. There my bright-eyed gipsy lass was waiting for me. A whispered colloquy ... a furtive glance or two up at this flat ... and you took the bait! Fired with the idea of catching me or my accomplice, you took up your vigil here, in this very flat, under the same roof as General Desroques and his faithful servant —Sylvestre Barnett! So that I was able to keep you under close observation, hear just what you were doing, and, through General Desroques, suggest to your receptive mind exactly such thoughts as I wanted to implant there."

Turning to the general, Jim Barnett gave the latter a glance of genuine admiration.

"I must tell you, general, that I cannot sufficiently commend your acting. You led Béchoux blindfold, step by step, towards our goal—namely, to find out the unknown constable's name, and then get him into this flat for a few minutes. Just a few minutes, Béchoux—not more. For the thing I was after was the same thing that you, the police, the State, and everyone else were after—that photograph!

"Knowing your industry, your ingenuity, your excessive energy in the pursuit of your duty, I realized that it would be useless to waste time going over ground you had already covered. What I had to do was to imagine the unimaginable—think of some utterly extraordinary and unheard-of hiding-place. I had to visualize it in advance, so that I could, if possible, possess myself of this secret receptacle on the day the constable came to the flat with you. And I had to obtain possession of it without his knowledge, for there wouldn't be time to search him, explore the linings of his clothes and the soles of his shoes, and so forth. And yet I *knew* that somewhere about his person he would have that photograph. The question was, where?

"I don't want to digress, but as soon as I knew the name of this constable of yours, Béchoux, I was considerably enlightened. The general's questions only confirmed what I already suspected—that this man, Rimbourg, was a clever fellow who, before he joined the police force, had had a distinctly varied experience and rather a checkered career! In short, I knew him to be just the man to hit upon some hiding-place so bold as to be unbelievable, so obvious as to seem fantastic! Something *he* could make use of, but which would never occur to anyone else as a possible place of concealment.

"Now, Béchoux, suppose we test the intelligence of the class. What is it that distinguishes a policeman on duty from a postman, a dustman, a railway porter, a fireman—in short, from every other kind of uniformed employee? Give it a moment's thought, while I count three. Your eagle intelligence will surely see it! One—two—three. Now, where was the hiding-place?"

Béchoux made no reply. Despite the disadvantage at which he found himself, he was trying desperately to snatch at this straw and guess the solution of the riddle, so apparent to the triumphant Barnett. But he could not for the life of him think what was the distinguishing characteristic of a policeman on duty.

"My poor friend," sympathized Barnett. "Out with the boys last night? Your brain seems a trifle dulled today. I don't usually have to enlighten you in words of one syllable only before you get your nose to the trail!"

But there was no rôle for Béchoux's nose to play in the incident which followed. Like a flash, Barnett darted out of the room, and returned a moment later gravely balancing on the tip of his own olfactory organ the shining baton—truncheon—nightstick—the same the wide world over, wielded by every police force, that bane of malefactors, that safeguard of life and property, that wooden club which has attained to the dignity of a symbol, and is able to break up the fiercest street-fight or halt the haughtiest limousine.

Barnett toyed with this particular baton like a music-hall juggler with a bottle. He let it slither down his nose, caught it, twirled it behind his leg, round his neck, and down his back. Before it could fall to the ground, he had grasped it again, and, holding it out between thumb and finger, he addressed it in accents of mock solemnity:

"O most honorable, most respectable, most admirable baton! Symbol of civic and municipal authority! A short while ago, you were hanging at Constable Rimbourg's belt. A little sleight of hand and, hey presto! another baton, your double hung in your place. You were left behind when the constable departed!" Béchoux started violently, but Barnett motioned him back to his seat. "He is unlikely to return to retrieve you. In fact, I doubt whether we shall ever hear from him again. His rôle in the drama is over; he filled it not unworthily. But you, O baton, will fulfil to the last *your* rôle of defender of those in distress, and from you we shall learn the secret of Jean Desroques and the beautiful Christiane Veraldy. Speak, little baton, I conjure you to speak!"

With his left hand Barnett seized firm hold of the handle, circled with narrow grooves. In his right, he held tightly the heavy body of the club, made of ash-wood, painted white, and attempted to twist it.

"I was right!" he exclaimed joyously. "But it's a miracle of workmanship. Not for nothing was Constable Rimbourg at one time a carpenter—the man must have been a master of his craft! See, he has hollowed out the heart of this club without ever breaking the outside, fixed this almost invisible channel for the screw, so that the two pieces of wood fit together so perfectly that there is no danger of the head of the club working loose."

Barnett gave the baton another twist. The handle came unscrewed, revealing a metal ring. The stick of the baton was now in two bits. In the longer section they could see a copper tube running the length of the club.

The faces of all three men wore expressions of rapt attention. They held their breath, so that the silence of the room was intensified. Despite himself, even Barnett was obviously impressed with the solemnity of the moment. He turned over the copper tubing, tapping it several times hard on the table. Out fell a roll of paper!

"That's it—the photograph!" murmured Béchoux.

"You recognize it, do you? It fits the official description all right. About six inches long, detached from its mount and rather crumpled. Will you kindly unroll it yourself, General Desroques?"

With trembling eagerness the general picked up the paper. His usually steady hand shook as he began unrolling the fateful scroll. There were four sheets of notepaper and a telegram pinned to the photograph. For a moment, the general stared in silence at the latter, then he showed it to the other two. In a voice vibrant with emotion he began speaking on a note of joy, which quickly gave place to one of grief.

"You see, it is the portrait of a woman. A young woman with a child on her lap. The face is that of Madame Veraldy—it tallies with the pictures in the press, except that here she is younger. This photograph must have been taken nine or ten years ago by the look of it. Yes; here's the date, in the bottom, left-hand corner. I was right. This picture is eleven years old. And it is signed 'Christiane'—Madame Veraldy's name!"

The general paused, then added thoughtfully:

"This establishes the fact that Jean must have known this woman in the past, possibly before her marriage to Veraldy."

"Read the letters, monsieur," suggested Barnett, handing over the first sheet, closely covered with fine, feminine handwriting.

General Desroques began reading. He had hardly read the first few lines, when he gave a kind of groan, as of a man who stumbles suddenly on a terrible and painful secret. Hurriedly he scanned the first letter, then, with increasing anxiety, turned to the others which, with the telegram, Barnett passed to him one by one.

"Can you tell us what you have found out, general?"

The general did not answer at once. His eyes were filled with tears when at last he muttered huskily:

"It is I who am to blame! I alone who am guilty.... About twelve years ago Jean fell in love with a little shop-girl. They had a baby, a boy. Jean wanted to marry his *amie*, but my heart was hardened by pride and snobbishness. I forbade the marriage and refused to see the girl. Jean was meaning to disobey me—for the first time—and marry her out of hand. But she would not let him. She sacrificed her own happiness so that my son should not quarrel with me. Here is her letter—the first one. She says: '*It's goodbye Jean. Your father won't let us get married. You must give in to him. If you don't it might mean bad luck for our darling baby.* [250]*I send you a picture of us both. Keep it always, and don't forget about us too soon....*'"

The general paused, overcome with emotion. He continued, more calmly:

"But it was she who forgot. Some time later she got engaged to Veraldy, then at the beginning of his career. Jean learned of their marriage, and had his little son brought up by a retired schoolmaster near Chartres. There the mother would sometimes visit him secretly."

Béchoux and Barnett were listening intently so as not to lose a word. It was not easy to follow the general's speech, as he dropped his voice until it was little more than a whisper. The hand that had held the letters trembled uncontrollably.

"The last letter," he continued, "is dated five months ago. It is very short. Christiane tells of her remorse and unhappiness. She is passionately fond of her child, and it is agony to her not to have him with her. Then comes the telegram, sent to Jean by the old schoolmaster: '*Child dangerously ill, come at once.*' At the bottom of the telegraph form are just these few words, scrawled by my son after the tragedy: '*Our child is dead. Christiane has killed herself.*'"

Again the general paused. No further explanations were needed. It was easy to guess what had happened. On receipt of the telegram, Jean had immediately sought out Christiane and taken her to the bedside of the dying child. On the way back to Paris, Christiane overcome with grief, had committed suicide.

"What shall we do about it?" Barnett wanted to know.

"We must reveal the truth," was the general's reply. "Jean's reasons for keeping silence are obvious. He was shielding the dead woman, but he also wanted to shield me, since I was really responsible for the terrible tragedy. Also, though he felt certain neither the schoolmaster at Chartres, nor Constable Rimbourg, who owed him a debt of gratitude, would betray him, he definitely did not want this conclusive piece of evidence to be destroyed. He wanted Fate to bring the truth to light. Now that you, Monsieur Barnett, have succeeded in effecting this revelation...."

"If I succeeded, general," said Barnett quickly, "it was solely due to the help of my friend, Béchoux. We mustn't lose sight of that. If Béchoux had not led us to Constable Rimbourg and his baton, I should have failed. It is Béchoux who deserves your thanks, general."

"My thanks are due to both of you," said the old soldier. "You have saved my son, and I shall not hesitate to do my duty."

Béchoux approved the general's decision. He was so deeply moved by what had just happened that he was even prepared to waive making any attempt to take possession of the documents the police were so urgently wanting. He was ready to take this course, although it meant sacrificing his personal prestige. His humanity triumphed over his professional conscience —not for the first time.

But as the general made to withdraw to his own room Béchoux stepped up to Barnett and tapped him on the shoulder with the curt words: "I arrest you, Jim Barnett!"

He spoke in the accents of sincerity. He was quite obviously going through what was a futile formality which he felt himself obliged to perform. He had instructions to arrest Barnett, and would do so, no matter what the circumstances.

Barnett held out his hand to the inspector.

"You win, Béchoux," he said, "you've arrested me, and carried out orders. Old Kaspar's work is done. And now, if you've no objection, I will make my escape. In that way our friendship will be saved and honor satisfied! You know I should do it anyway."

Béchoux shook the outstretched hand of his strange friend with heartfelt warmth. Between these two alternately allies and enemies, a truce was called—perhaps even a permanent amnesty. Both men recalled with genuine emotion their former encounters, the adventures they had experienced in company.

Béchoux expressed his feelings with that characteristic blunt simplicity that made him so popular with his colleagues and the world at large.

"You're the greatest of all of them, Barnett. You stand absolutely alone. Your feat today is nothing short of miraculous. No one but you could have solved the puzzle!"

"I don't know," said Barnett reflectively. "After all, I had that inkling of Rimbourg's past to help me. Do you know the man had actually worked for an illusionist and conjurer at one time. And his little idea in joining the police force was probably mainly the advantage of being in close proximity to the pickings on every possible occasion. Although he demonstrated unwavering loyalty to his benefactor, Jean Desroques, we must not lose sight of Rimbourg's real character. He was a policeman, much as you suspect me of being a detective——"

Béchoux cut him short.

"None of that now," he cried. "Oh, but you're a wonder. Who on earth but you would ever have discovered such an improbable hiding-place as the inside of a police baton?"

Barnett cocked his head on one side and simpered unbecomingly in imitation of a blushing schoolgirl.

"Any one's wits are sharper when there is a prize at stake."

"A prize? How do you mean? Surely you're not thinking of any reward General Desroques may offer you? You must know he's not at all well off."

"And if he did offer me anything, I should have to refuse it. You mustn't forget the proud motto of the Barnett Agency. No fees of any kind—services gratis—we work for glory!"

"Well, then...." Inspector Béchoux looked distinctly puzzled; worried, too. Barnett smiled guilelessly.

"The fact is, as I was glancing quickly through the fourth letter before passing it to the general, I saw that it stated Christiane Veraldy had from the outset told her husband of her past! Consequently, the banker was fully cognizant of his wife's former love affair, and knew that she had a child! Yet he deliberately neglected to inform the police of these facts. This he did out of jealousy and in the hope that his silence might bring Jean Desroques to the scaffold. He knew that Desroques would never reveal the dead woman's secret.

"You will agree that this was a pretty blackguardly thing to do. Now don't you think that, with all his money, Veraldy would be prepared to come down handsomely in order to prevent that letter becoming public property? Don't you think that if some trustworthy, respectable man— Sylvestre, for instance, General Desroques' servant—were to go to Veraldy and offer quite spontaneously to hand over that piece of paper, the banker would be prepared to talk business? I am taking a chance on being right in my supposition, as I was about the police baton, for instance. In fact, just so as to be able to play my hunch I slipped the letter into my pocket!"

Béchoux groaned. It was all wrong, of course. And yet, it seemed only fair that Barnett should reap some reward for the exercise of his special deductive skill. The laborer is worthy of his hire. And if the innocent were saved and wrongs were righted, what objection could there really be to those "commissions" Barnett habitually extracted from the pockets of the guilty parties in a case?

"*Au revoir*, Barnett," said the inspector, shaking hands again. And at the back of his mind lurked the certainty that next time he had a knotty problem to tackle he would be quite ready to compromise with his scruples and call in Barnett's invaluable aid.

"*Au revoir*, Béchoux," said Barnett. "I shall be ringing you up in a day or so, I expect."

"What about?"

"You'll know all in good time," and Jim Barnett was off and away.

CHAPTER XI

AFTERWORD

"Hallo! I want to speak to Chief Inspector Béchoux!"

It was Barnett's voice on the line.

"*Inspector* Béchoux speaking," replied Béchoux coldly. "Is that some one trying to be funny?"

"Oh, Béchoux, don't tell me you haven't recognized my voice. After all this while! And I thought you loved me!"

"Oh, it's you, Barnett? Well, if you're just fooling, you may as well ring off. I'm busy."

"But I've good news for you, old chap!" Barnett's tone grew distinctly plaintive.

Inspector Béchoux thawed a trifle.

"What is it, then?" he asked.

"Although you failed to get Arsène Lupin as you swore you would, or to get that photograph as per instructions, yet Fate smiles on you. Isn't it lovely? I've put in such a good word for you with the people higher up, and shown them so clearly what remarkable services you rendered to the cause of justice in that Desroques case, that they are going to appoint you a Chief Inspector. Oh, don't thank me! Merely a trifling mark of my esteem. From Barnett to Béchoux, as it were, in memory of many happy days. And now at last my conscience is at rest, for you, too, have reaped the fruit of our alliance in those adventures where I was privileged to intervene!"

And Béchoux felt oddly pleased that his promotion, albeit well deserved, should have come through Barnett. He reflected that it took a man like Barnett to make a vast organization like the police force recognize the merits of one of the minor cogs in the machine. Nevertheless he had no doubts at all of the altogether special merits of one Inspector Béchoux and his eminent suitability for promotion!

Therefore it was in a spirit of unfeigned and unclouded gratitude, but not altogether of surprise, that he answered now:

"Thank you, thank you, Barnett. The appointment will mean twice as much to me, coming as it does through you!"

Inspector Béchoux had set out to arrest Arsène Lupin—and had ended by becoming himself a prisoner of Jim Barnett's brains!